The Mourning Thief
and Other Stories

ff

THE
MOURNING
THIEF
and other stories

Desmond Hogan

faber and faber
LONDON · BOSTON

This collection first published in 1987
by Faber and Faber Limited
3 Queen Square London WC1n 3au

'The Last Time', 'Afternoon', 'Embassy', 'Portrait of a Dancer', 'A Poet and
an Englishman', 'Jimmy' and 'The Birth of Laughter' were first published in
Diamonds at the Bottom of the Sea by Hamish Hamilton in 1979. 'The Man from
Korea', 'The Sojourner', 'Memories of Swinging London' and 'Teddyboys'
were first published in *Children of Lir* by Hamish Hamilton in 1981.

Photoset by Wilmaset Birkenhead Wirral
Printed in Great Britain by
Richard Clay Ltd Bungay Suffolk
All rights reserved

British Library Cataloguing in Publication Data

Hogan, Desmond
The mourning thief and other stories.
I. Title
823'.914 [F]   PR6058.0346
ISBN 0–571–15015–2

For Maryanne and Jessica and Jan

Ring out the want, the care, the sin,
The faithless coldness of the times.

                                        Tennyson

Acknowledgements

Acknowledgements are made to the following:

To *Bananas* for 'Teddyboys'; to the Irish Press, *New Irish Writing* and Verlag Volk and Weit, Berlin, for 'The Last Time'; to *Bananas* for 'The Man from Korea'; to Longship Press and Wolfhound for 'A Poet and an Englishman' from *Paddy No More*; to *Company* for 'Portrait of a Dancer'; to Hamish Hamilton for 'The Birth of Laughter' published in *Irish Ghost Stories*, edited by Joseph Hone; to Adam International for 'Memories of Swinging London'; to *Time Out* for 'The Sojourner'; and to the *New Statesman* for 'The Mourning Thief'.

   Some of these stories won the John Llewellyn Rhys Memorial Prize.

Contents

Teddyboys

With a curious sultry look they waited, diamonds in their eyes, and handkerchiefs, thick and scarlet, in their pockets. They stood around, lying against the bank corner, shouldering some extraordinary responsibility, keeping imagination, growth, hope alive in a small Irish town some time around the beginning of the sixties.

Then mysteriously they disappeared; all but one, Jamesy Clarke, gone to Birmingham, London, leaving one solitary teddyboy to hoist his red carnation. It was a lovely spring when they left. I was sorry they'd gone. But there was Jamesy.

He bit his lip with a kind of sullen spite. His eyes glinted, topaz. His hair gleamed. His shirts were scarlet and his tie blue with white polka dots.

As spring came early young men dived into the weir.

I wanted, against this background of river teeming with salmon, to congratulate Jamesy Clarke for staying to keep the spirit of dashing dress and sultry eyes alive. Instead I followed him, ever curious, watching each step he took, knowing him to be unusually beautiful and somewhat beloved by the Gods. Though nine years of age, going on ten, I knew about these Gods. An old fisherman by the Suck had once said, 'The Gods always protect those who are doomed.' I harboured this information. I told no one.

Jamesy had stayed to look after his widowed mother. He lived in the 'Terrace' with her, behind a huge sign for Guinness, bottles abandoned, usually broken, children running about, a cry and a whine rising from them that aggravated the nerves and haunted like other signs of poverty haunted, dolls broken and destroyed, old men leaning against the men's lavatory, drunken and abused. His mother was allegedly dying from an unspoken disease, sitting among statues of Mary, that surrounded her like meringues, and cough-bottle smelling irises.

I'd never actually seen his mother. But I knew she dominated the tone of Jamesy's life, the prayers, the supplications, the calling on Our Lady of Fatima. Our Lady of Fatima was very popular in our town. She adorned most houses, in some more agonized than others, and a remarkable statement under her in my aunt's house: 'Eventually my pure heart will prevail.'

The fields about the river were radiant with buttercups, fluff amassed and fled over the Green and odd youngsters swam. I noticed Jamesy swimming a few times, always by himself, always when evening came, taking off his clothes, laying them in the stillness, jumping into the water in scarlet trunks. He never saw me. He wasn't supposed to. Like a little emissary of the Gods I wandered about, taking note, keeping check, always acute and waiting for any circumstance which could do him harm. He was much too precious to me. His shirts, scarlet and blue, impressed me more than Walt Disney movies. But it was his eyes that awed me more than anything, eyes faraway as the Connemara mountains and yet near, near in sympathy and in sensation, eyes that saw and kept their distance.

Scandal broke like mouldy Guinness when apparently Jamesy was caught in the launderette making love to a girl. The girl was whizzed off to England. Clouds of June gathered; the Elizabethan fortress by the river stood out, one of the last outposts of the Queen in Connaught. Jamesy kept his distance. He didn't seem troubled or disturbed by scandal. He went his way. It was as though this girl was like washing on the line. She hadn't altered his life, hadn't changed him.

He smoked cigarettes by the bank corner, alone there now. Their scents accumulated in my nostrils. I took to naming cigarettes like one would flowers. A mantra rose in my mind that ordered and preoccupied a summer: Gipsy Annie, Sailor Tim. I called cigarette brands new names. I exploited all the knowledge I had of the perverse and applied it to Jamesy's cigarettes.

Ancient women sold pike in the Square. Sometimes they looked to the sky. They'd never seen a summer like this, broken cloud, imminent heat.

Old men wiped their foreheads and engrossed people in conversation about the Black and Tans. Everything harkened back; to the Rising, to the War of Independence, to the Civil War. Forgotten heroes and cowards were discussed and debated. The mental hospital looked particularly threatening; as though at any moment it was going to lurch out and grab. Jamesy swam. He had no part in conversation about the rising, in talk of new jobs or new factories. Where he was financed from I don't know but he led a beautiful life and if it hadn't been for him the summer would not have been exciting and I would not have eagerly waited for the holidays when I could follow him along the railway tracks, always at a distance, until he came to a different part of the river from the one he swam in, sitting there, thinking.

When he started going out with a tailor's daughter I was horrified. I knew by the way she dressed she did not have his sense of colour. She walked with an absence of dignity. His arm always hung on her shoulder in a half-hearted way and she led him away from the familiar spots, the bank corner, the river.

I saw them go to a film. I observed him desert the summer twilights. I felt like writing to his friends in England, asking them to come back and send him out or feeding his mother with poison to make her complaint worse. Even the hold his mother's disease had on him seemed negligible in comparison to this girl's.

I noticed the actresses who starred in the film they went to see, Audrey Hepburn, Lana Turner, and privately held them responsible. I looked up at Lana Turner one night when they'd entered the cinema and told her I would put a curse on her.

I learnt about curses from a mad stocky aunt who lived in the country, was once regarded with affection by all our family until an uncle had a mongoloid child. Then attention diverted from her and she started cursing everyone, making dolls of them and putting them in fields of corn. I knew it worked. About the time she did one on my mother, my mother went to hospital. I knew it was an awful thing to do. But there was too much at stake.

The more I cursed her though, the more defiant Lana Turner looked, her breasts seemed almost barer. I stopped cursing her and started swearing at her, swearing at her out loud. The local curate passed. He looked at me. I said, 'Hello Father.'

He wondered at a child staring at a poster of Lana Turner, calling her by all the foul names my father called my mother.

Come July young men basked by the river. The sun had broken through and an element of ecstasy had come to town, towels, bottles of orange thrown about. Ivy grew thick and dirty about the Elizabethan fortress, gnats made their home there and a royal humming commenced then, a humming and a distillation of the voices of gnats and flies.

The evenings were wild and crimson; clouds raged like different brands of lipstick. That's one thing I'll say for Jamesy Clarke, he still took the odd swim by himself. In the silence after twilight he took off his clothes and dived into the water. Threads were whispered over the grass by the spiders. Wet descended. The splash of water reverberated. There were moments of silence when he just urged through the water. I waited across the field, my head in my lap. If I could I would have built him a golden bridge out of here. I knew all that was piled against him, class, the time that was in it, his mother. It no longer mattered to me that this town should have him. What I wanted for him was a future in which he could puff on smart cigarettes in idyllic circumstances. But much as I racked my brain I could think of nowhere to place him. London and Birmingham sounded too dour, Fatima was already peopled by statues of the Blessed Virgin and other places I knew of I was uncertain of, Paris, Rome. There just might have been a place for him in Hollywood but I knew him to be too elegant for it, there were more than likely simpler and more beautiful places in the United States into which he could have fitted. I wanted him more than anything to be safe, though safe from what I didn't know.

He held his girlfriend's hand about town. He sat on the fair green with her. He hugged her to him. He'd discarded jackets and wore orange T-shirts. A bracelet banded his arm, narrowly scathing hairs on his skin which was the colour of hot honey. I looked to the sky above them, clouds like rockets in it. Perhaps his girlfriend did have something after all, a hunch of his existence. Nobody could have seduced him for so much time away from bank corner or river without responding to something in him. I forgave her. I gave up ownership. I played with the notion of being present at their marriage. I had it already arranged in my mind. He'd be dressed in white. She in blue. There'd be marigolds as there were outside the courthouse and his mother, virtually dead, would be in a movable bed in the church.

Then one day things changed. The weather broke. Clouds which had been threatening, sending shadows coursing over wheat and water, now plunged into rain. The heat evaporated and a sudden cold absorbed all that was beautiful, warmth in old stone, the preening of daisies in sidewalk crevices. I shook inside. I had to stay in. I played with dinkies. I looked through books. I found no information relevant to life. I burnt a total of three books one evening, two about horses and one an adventure story set in Surrey. I became like a little censor, impatient and ravaging anything that didn't immediately allow one in on the mystery of being. Dickens was merely sent back to the library. He was lucky.

I wrote a letter to Jamesy; he stood stranded by rain.

Dear Jamesy,
   I hate the rain. I wish I lived in a country where it didn't rain. How are you? I'm not too well.
   I've decided I don't like books anymore. I prefer things like clothes. My mother keeps giving out. She was giving out when the sun was shining and she gives out when it's raining. How's your mother? I said a prayer to Our Lady of Fatima for her yesterday.
   It's raining outside now. I'm going to draw a picture of Mecca. I was just reading about Mecca where all the Moslems go. I'm going to draw a picture of it and colour it in. See you soon I hope.

Desmond.

I didn't send the letter of course. I coloured it in too, drawing pictures of teddyboys along the sides. I also drew a scarlet heart, pierced by an arrow, the number three, emphasizing it in blue, and a tree trunk.

I bore it with me for a while until one day it fell out of my pocket, the colours washing into the rain.

Jamesy had had a row with his girlfriend. That was obvious when the sun shone again. He looked disgruntled. An old woman, member of a myriad confraternities, reported that he spat on the pavement in front of her. 'Disgusting,' the lady said. 'Disgusting,' my mother agreed. 'A cur,' the lady said. 'A cur,' my mother said. And the lady added, 'What do you expect from the likes of him. His eyes,' she screeched with outrage, 'his beady eyes.'

It was true. Jamesy's eyes had changed, become pained, narrow, fallen from grace. He wore a white jacket, always clean though in his despair, and his features knotted in disgruntlement as cold winds blew and a flotsam of old ladies wandered the town, gossiping, discussing all shapes of misdemeanour with one another in highly pitched, off-centre voices.

Jamesy edged into the voice of autumn, his dislocation, his pain, and his eyes spitting, a venom in them now.

He began seeing his girlfriend again. This time he tugged her about town. She was a vehicle he pushed and swayed. Though a tailor's daughter she had her good points, grace I had to admit, and an almond colour in her hair, always combed and arranged to a kind of exactitude.

Lana Turner never graced our cinema again. There were posters which showed motorcycles or men in leather jackets, their faces screwed up as they unleashed a punch on someone. I lost Jamesy on his trail more than often.

Women whispered about Our Lady of Fatima now as though she was threatening them. Voices spoke of death, a faint shell-shocked murmuring each time a member of the community passed away. Death was wed into our town like a sister, a nucleus about which to whisper, a kind of alley-way to the Divine.

Almost as suddenly as it went, the fine weather returned, revealing a curious harvest, tractors in the fields, farmers, brown as river slime, on bicycles. Then young men of town returned to the river. They were quieter now, something was pulling out of their lives, summer, imperceptibly, like a tide.

Northern Protestants had come and gone, daubing a poster on the mill overlooking the weir, 'What shall it profit a man; if he shall gain the whole world, and lose his own soul?'

I couldn't find Jamesy. There was no sign of him in the evenings, swimming. I started an odyssey, seeking him through field and wood. Birds called. I thought I heard Indians once or twice. Horses lazed about, the last flowers of summer sung with bees, standing above the grass, lime and gold. The bold lettering of the poster above the weir was in my mind, its message was absent. I did not understand it.

My travels led me to wood and to Georgian house lying outside the town. I hadn't forgotten Jamesy but I kept looking, pretending to myself I'd see him in far-flung places.

I sat on a hill one day and looked at the river beyond. My T-shirt was red. My mind was tranquil. I used the moment to think of Jamesy, his eyes, his anguish. I had seen that anguish cutting into his face in the course of the summer, into his eyes, his cheekbones, his mouth. I had seen a sculpture gradually realizing itself and the sculpture, like beautiful stamps, like stained glass in the church, spoke of an element of human nature I did not understand but knew was there, grief. It was manifest in Jamesy. I wondered about his mother, her journey towards death, his attitude to it, his solitary trails about town, the manifold cigarettes, the grimaces.

I imagined his mother's bedroom as I had visualized it many times, one statue standing out among the statues of Mary, that of Our Lady of Fatima, notable for her beauty and the snake writhing at her feet. That snake I identified now as a curse, the one that blighted Jamesy's face, the one that blighted Ireland, trodden on by the benign feet of one whose purity might as she claimed ultimately prevail.

My searching for Jamesy was becoming more spurious, a kind of game now, an unspoken fantasy; gone was the grandeur of odyssey. I observed thicket, nettle and flower.

Then one evening late in August unexpectedly I came on Jamesy. It was virtually dark, by the river, letters standing out on the poster, and as I wandered by the Elizabethan fortress noise became apparent to me. I looked over a hedge. There in the grass by a tributary of the river Jamesy was making love to the tailor's daughter.

The skirmish of a bird with a bush could not have been more noiseless than me, the running of an otter in the grass. I made my way home, shaken by what I had seen.

I hated him, yet I hated him with a hatred that transcended Jamesy. I hated him for what he was doing, for the image he had given me, for this new distortion on stained glass.

I wanted to share his simplicity, an empathy with his face. But there was more to him than a face and in the silence of my room, a wind rushing on the river outside as swans flew over, in the tradition of my rural aunt, in the tradition of gipsies and the country Irish people rummaging with broken dolls, I cursed Jamesy.

He should not have told me what I didn't want to know, that the human spirit is tarnished.

8

Jamesy's girlfriend left town, a silent pageant by the station, she was going to a job in Dublin. He was there to say goodbye to her, a teddyboy on a summer day, platform shorn of all but marigolds. I watched him now, assisting him towards his doom.

He swam again in summer evenings alone, silently racing across dew moistened grass to dive into the water and one evening when I wasn't looking he was drowned.

I wanted to tell everyone it was me who did it, I wanted to announce my guilt and be penalized for it. But in my T-shirt red as a balloon in the late summer radiance no one listened; I was denied any sense of retribution. I was ignored.

His funeral occurred two days before I returned to school. Young girls with the look of girls from the 'Terrace', faces pinched and yet knowledgeable, marched behind a hearse piled with masses of red carnations. He had many cousins, young females, and thereby many wreaths were donated.

The town came out in throngs, people loving funerals, and he being young, they accepted his death, excusing him all, his background, his spitting on the cement as he passed old ladies.

'Sure he stayed to look after his mother,' women slurred, and his mother, risen from her deathbed, looking fine and healthy, was there, a woman in black with a scarf of emerald and white on her head.

The prayers were read; a woman of the community, respectable, stood out from the crowd, a single tear in her eye.

Glass was reflected around the cemetery, domes bearing images of the sky and other wreaths and when they were all gone I stayed.

I knew he had departed for ever, his death seemed inevitable like so many things, autumn, and the poster on the weir.

I told him I was sorry. I apologized. I knew, however, the grief of his death would fill my life and whether I was responsible or not I'd always see him wherever I went, his eyes, his tie with the colonnade of polka dots.

His mother assumed perfect health in the next few months, whether assisted by Our Lady of Fatima or not I'll never know, but one thing I understood, over school books, in the anguish of the classroom I knew by looking out the window that somehow she had triumphed as she said she would. The lady with iron eyes, blue drapes on her robe, her hands joined in prayer and her feet squelching a snake, had prevailed.

Our Lady of Fatima, touchstone of the miraculous, had claimed unto herself a soul before it knew the damp of winter or the drought that issued from the human heart.

The Last Time

The last time I saw him was in Ballinasloe station, 1953, his long figure hugged into a coat too big for him. Autumn was imminent; the sky grey, baleful. A few trees had become grey too; God, my heart ached. The tennis court beyond, silent now, the river close, half-shrouded in fog. And there he was, Jamesy, tired, knotted, the doctor's son who took me out to the pictures once, courted me in the narrow timber seats as horns played in a melodramatic forties film.

Jamesy had half the look of a mongol, half the look of an autistic child, blond hair parted like waves of water reeds, face salmon-colour, long, the shade and colour of autumnal drought. His father had a big white house on the perimeter of town – doors and windows painted as fresh as crocuses and lawns gloomy and yet blanched with perpetually new-mown grass.

In my girlhood I observed Jamesy as I walked with nuns and other orphans by his garden. I was an orphan in the local convent, our play-fields stretching by the river at the back of elegant houses where we watched the nice children of town, bankers' children, doctors' children, playing. Maria Mulcahy was my name. My mother, I was told in later years, was a Jean Harlow-type prostitute from the local terraces. I, however, had hair of red which I admired in the mirror in the empty, virginal-smelling bathroom of the convent hall where we sat with children of doctors and bankers who had to pay three pence into the convent film show to watch people like Joan Crawford marry in bliss.

Jamesy was my first love, a distant love.

11

In his garden he'd be cutting hedges or reading books, a face on him like an interested hedgehog. The books were big and solemn-looking – like himself. Books like *War and Peace*, I later discovered.

Jamesy was the bright boy, though his father wanted him to do dentistry.

He was a problem child, it was well known. When I was seventeen I was sent to a draper's house to be a maid, and there I gathered information about Jamesy. The day he began singing 'Bye Bye Blackbird' in the church, saying afterwards he was singing it about his grandmother who'd taken a boat one day, sailed down the river until the boat crashed over a weir and the woman drowned. Another day he was found having run away, sleeping on a red bench by the river where later we wrote our names, sleeping with a pet fox, for foxes were abundant that year.

Jamesy and I met first in the fair green. I was wheeling a child and in a check shirt he was holding a rabbit. The green was spacious, like a desert. *Duel in the Sun* was showing in town and the feeling between us was one of summer and space, the grass rich and twisted like an old nun's hair.

He smiled crookedly.

I addressed him.

'I know you!' I was blatant, tough. He laughed.

'You're from the convent.'

'I'm working now!'

'Have a sweet!'

'I don't eat them. I'm watching my figure!'

'Hold the child!'

I lifted the baby out, rested her in his arms, took out a rug and sat down. Together we watched the day slip, the sun steadying. I talked about the convent and he spoke about *War and Peace* and an uncle who'd died in the Civil War, torn apart by horses, his arms tied to their hooves.

'He was buried with the poppies,' Jamesy said. And as though to remind us, there were sprays of poppies on the fair green, distant, distrustful.

12

'What age are you?'

'Seventeen! Do you see my rabbit?'

He gave it to me to hold. Dumb-bells, he called it. There was a fall of hair over his forehead and by bold impulse I took it and shook it fast.

There was a smile on his face like a pleased sheep. 'I'll meet you again,' I said as I left, pushing off the pram as though it held billycans rather than a baby.

There he was that summer, standing on the bridge by the prom, sitting on a park bench or pawing a jaded copy of Turgenev's *Fathers and Sons*.

He began lending me books and under the pillow I'd read Zola's *Nana* or a novel by Marie Corelli, or maybe poetry by Tennyson. There was always a moon that summer – or a very red sunset. Yet I rarely met him, just saw him. Our relationship was blindly educational, little else. There at the bridge, a central point, beside which both of us paused, at different times, peripherally. There was me, the pram, and he in a shirt that hung like a king's cloak, or on cold days – as such there often were – in a jumper which made him look like a polar bear.

'I hear you've got a good voice,' he told me one day.

'Who told you?'

'I heard.'

'Well, I'll sing you a song.' I sang. 'Somewhere over the Rainbow', which I'd learnt at the convent.

Again we were in the green. In the middle of singing the song I realized my brashness and also my years of loneliness, destitution, at the hands of nuns who barked and crowded about the statue of the Infant Jesus of Prague in the convent courtyard like seals on a rock. They hadn't been bad, the nuns. Neither had the other children been so bad. But God, what loneliness there'd been. There'd been one particular tree there, open like a complaint, where I spent a lot of time surveying the river and the reeds, waiting for pirates or for some beautiful lady straight out of a Veronica Lake movie to come sailing up the river. I began weeping in the green that day, weeping loudly. There was his face which I'll never forget. Jamesy's face changed from blank idiocy, local precociousness, to a sort of wild understanding.

He took my hand.

I leaned against his jumper; it was a fawn colour.

I clumsily clung to the fawn and he took me and I was aware of strands of hair, bleached by sun.

The Protestant church chimed five and I reckoned I should move, pushing the child ahead of me. The face of Jamesy Murphy became more intense that summer, his pink colour changing to brown. He looked like a pirate in one of the convent film shows, tanned, ravaged.

Yet our meetings were just as few and as autumn denuded the last of the cherry-coloured leaves from a particular house-front on the other side of town, Jamesy and I would meet by the river, in the park – briefly, each day, touching a new part of one another. An ankle, a finger, an ear lobe, something as ridiculous as that. I always had a child with me so it made things difficult.

Always too I had to hurry, often racing past closing shops.

There were Christmas trees outside a shop one day I noticed, so I decided Christmas was coming. Christmas was so unreal now, an event remembered from convent school, huge Christmas pudding and nuns crying. Always on Christmas Day nuns broke down crying, recalling perhaps a lost love or some broken-hearted mother in an Irish kitchen.

Jamesy was spending a year between finishing at school and his father goading him to do dentistry, reading books by Joyce now and Chekhov, and quoting to me one day – overlooking a garden of withered dahlias – Nijinsky's diaries. I took books from him about writers in exile from their countries, holding under my pillow novels by obscure Americans.

There were high clouds against a low sky that winter and the grotesque shapes of the Virgin in the alcove of the church, but against that monstrosity the romance was complete I reckon, an occasional mad moon, Lili Marlene on radio –

memories of a war that had only grazed childhood – a peacock feather on an ascendancy-type lady's hat.

'Do you see the way that woman's looking at us,' Jamesy said one day. Yes, she was looking at him as though he were a monster. His reputation was complete: a boy who was spoilt, daft, and an embarrassment to his parents. And there was I, a servant girl, talking to him. When she'd passed we embraced – lightly – and I went home, arranging to see him at the pictures the following night.

Always our meetings had occurred when I brushed past Jamesy with the pram. This was our first night out, seeing that Christmas was coming and that bells were tinkling on radio; we'd decided we'd be bold. I'd sneak out at eight o'clock, having pretended to go to bed. What really enticed me to ask Jamesy to bring me to the pictures was the fact that he was wearing a new Aran sweater and that I heard the film was partly set in Marrakesh, a place that had haunted me ever since I had read a book about where a heroine and two heroes met their fatal end in that city.

So things went as planned until the moment when Jamesy and I were in one another's arms when the woman for whom I worked came in, hauled me off. Next day I was brought before Sister Ignatius. She sat like a robot in the Spanish Inquisition. I was removed from the house in town and told I had to stay in the convent.

In time a job washing floors was found for me in Athlone, a neighbouring town to which I got a train every morning. The town was a drab one, replete with spires.

I scrubbed floors, my head wedged under heavy tables: sometimes I wept. There were Sacred Heart pictures to throw light on my predicament but even they were of no avail to me; religion was gone in a convent hush. Jamesy now was lost, looking out of a window I'd think of him but like the music of Glenn Miller he was past. His hair, his face, his madness I'd hardly touched, merely fondled like a floating ballerina.

It had been a mute performance – like a circus clown.

There'd been something I wanted of Jamesy which I'd never reached; I couldn't put words or emotions to it but now from a desk in London, staring into a Battersea dawn, I see it was a womanly feeling. I wanted love.

'Maria, you haven't cleaned the lavatory.' So with a martyred air I cleaned the lavatory and my mind dwelt on Jamesy's pimples, ones he had for a week in September.

The mornings were drab and grey. I'd been working a year in Athlone, mind disconnected from body, when I learned Jamesy was studying dentistry in Dublin. There was a world of difference between us, a partition as deep as war and peace. Then one morning I saw him. I had a scarf on and a slight breeze was blowing and it was the aftermath of a sullen summer and he was returning to Dublin. He didn't look behind. He stared – almost at the tracks – like a fisherman at the sea.

I wanted to say something but my clothes were too drab; not the nice dresses of two years before, dresses I'd resurrected from nowhere with patterns of sea-lions or some such thing on them.

'Jamesy Murphy, you're dead,' I said – my head reeled.

'Jamesy Murphy, you're dead.'

I travelled on the same train with him as far as Athlone. He went on to Dublin. We were in different carriages.

I suppose I decided that morning to take my things and move, so in a boat full of fat women bent on paradise I left Ireland.

I was nineteen and in love. In London through the auspices of the Sisters of Mercy in Camden Town I found work in an hotel where my red hair looked ravishing, sported over a blue uniform.

In time I met my mate, a handsome handy building contractor from Tipperary, whom I married – in the pleased absence of relatives – and with whom I lived in Clapham, raising children, he getting a hundred pounds a week, working seven days a week. My hair I carefully tended and wore heavy check shirts. We never went back to Ireland. In fact, we've never gone back to Ireland since I left, but occasionally, wheeling a child into the Battersea fun-fair, I was reminded of Jamesy, a particular strand of hair blowing across his face. Where was he? Where was the hurt and that face and the sensitivity? London was flooding with dark people and there at the beginning of the sixties I'd cross Chelsea bridge, walk my children up by Cheyne Walk, sometimes waiting to watch a candle lighting. Gradually it became more real to me that I loved him, that we were active within a certain sacrifice. Both of us had been bare and destitute when we met. The two of us had warded off total calamity, total loss. 'Jamesy!' His picture swooned; he was like a ravaged corpse in my head and the area between us opened; in Chelsea library I began reading books by Russian authors. I began loving him again. A snatch of Glenn Miller fell across the faded memory of colours in the rain, lights of the October fair week in Ballinasloe, Ireland.

The world was exploding with young people – protests against nuclear bombs were daily reported – but in me the nuclear area of the town where I'd worked returned to me.

Jamesy and I had been the marchers, Jamesy and I had been the protest! 'I like your face,' Jamesy once said to me. 'It looks like you could blow it away with a puff.'

In Chelsea library I smoked cigarettes though I wasn't supposed to. I read Chekhov's biography and Turgenev's biography – my husband minding the children – and tried to decipher an area of loss, a morning by the station, summer gone.

I never reached him; I just entertained him like as a child in an orphanage in the west of Ireland I had held a picture of Claudette Colbert under my pillow to remind me of glamour. The gulf between me and Jamesy narrows daily. I address him in a page of a novel, in a chip shop alone at night or here now, writing to you, I say something I never said before, something I've never written before.

I touch upon truth.

The Man from Korea

Afterwards it had the awkward grace of a legend; a silence when his name was mentioned, an implied understanding of what had happened. Few know what actually happened though, so to make it easier for you to understand I will make my own version.

I was five when he came to town, a child at street corners. I was an intensely curious child, a seer, one who poked into everyone's houses and recalled scandal, chagrin and disgrace. I know all about the Hennessys and if I don't let me pretend to.

He came in 1956. He was a young man of twenty-nine but already there was something old about him. He recalled the fires of the Korean war. He'd been an American pilot there. I'm not sure what he saw but it left his face with a curious neglect of reality; he stared ahead. Sometimes a donkey, a flying piece of hay, a budding tree at the end of the street would enthral him but otherwise silence. He kept quiet. He kept his distance. He shared very few things but he talked much to me. By a fire in the Hennessys', flames spitting and crying out, he talked of the sacred places of Asia, shrines to draconian goddesses, seated statues of Buddha.

I always nodded with understanding.

I suppose that's why he trusted me. Because, although a child of five, I was used to lengthy conversations with fire brigade men, painters, road-sweepers. So he and I discussed Buddha, Korea and sunsets which made you forget war, long raving sunsets, sunsets of ruby and a red brushed but not destroyed by orange. The air became red for odd moments in Korea; the redness stood in the air, so much so you could almost ensnare a colour.

He had blond hair, sharpened by glints of silver and gold, a face tainted by a purple colour. It was as though someone had painted him, brush strokes running through his appearance, a glow, a healthiness about it, yet always a malign image before his eyes that kept him quiet, that compelled an austerity into eyes that would otherwise have been lit by handsomeness in the middle of a strange, arresting and, for an Irish small town, very distinctive face.

He came in April, time when the hedgerows were blossoming, time when tinkers moved on and anglers serenely stood above the river. Light rains penetrated his arrival; talk of fat trout and drone of drovers in the pub next door to the Hennessys in the evening.

The Hennessys were the most auspicious young ladies in town. Margaret and Mona. They'd been left a small fortune by a father who won the Irish Sweep Stakes once and the pools another time. Their father had spent his whole life gambling. His wife had left him in the middle of it all. But before he died he won large stakes of money and these passed to his daughters. So his life wasn't in vain. They made sure of that, gambling and feasting themselves, an accordion moving through the night, taking all into its rhythms, sound of a train, flash of a bicycle light. The Hennessy girls sported and sang, inflaming passions of spinsters, rousing priests like devils, but retaining this in their sitting room, a knowledge of joy, a disposition for good music and songs that weren't loud and sluttish but graced by magic. Such were the songs I heard from bed up the road, songs about the Irish heart for ever misplaced and wandering on Broadway or in Sydney, Australia, miles from home, but sure of this, its heritage of bog, lake and Irish motherhood.

The Hennessys had no mother; she'd gone early but their house was opened as a guest-house before their father won his fortunes and so it continued, despite money and all, less a guest-house, more a hospice for British anglers and Irish circus artistes. One travelling painter with a circus painted the Rock of Cashel on the wall. A fire blazed continually in the back room and the sweetness of hawthorn reigned.

You don't bring hawthorn into the house, it's bad luck; but the Hennessys had no mind for superstition and their house smelt of hedgerow, was smitten by sound of distant train, and warmed by a turf fire. Karl came to this house in 1956.

He meant to stay for a few weeks. His stay lasted the summer and if he did go early in autumn it was only because there was hurt in his stay.

The girls at first kept their distance, served him hot tea, brown bread, Chivers marmalade. He spent a lot of time by the fire, not just staring into it but regulating his thoughts to the outbursts of flame. He had seen war and one was aware of that; he was making a composition from war, images of children mowed down and buildings in flame. He came from a far country and had been in another far country. He was a stranger, an ex-soldier, but he was capable of recognizing the images of the world he hailed from in the flames of a fire in a small town in Ireland. I suppose that's why people liked him. He had the touch, just the touch of a poet.

Margaret and Mona nursed him like a patient; making gestures towards his solitude, never venturing too far but the tone of their house altering; the parties easing out and a meditativeness coming, two girls staring into a fire, recalling their lives.

Their father had brought them up, a man in a coffee-coloured suit, white shirt always open. They'd been pretty girls with ribbons like banners on their heads. Their father would bring them to the bog, bring them to picnics by the river, bring them on outings to Galway. Not a very rich man, he was rent collector, but eventually won all around him and left them wealthy.

Karl when he came sat alone a lot, walked the limestone street, strolled by the river. His shirt, like their father's, was white and open-necked, his suit, when he wore it, granite grey but more than often he wore jeans and shirts, dragon-red with squares of black on them.

Even his eyebrows were blond, coming to a sudden quiz-zical halt.

He often smoked a cigarette as though it was a burden. Sometimes a bird seemed to shock him or a fish leaping with a little quiver of jubilation. The mayfly came, the continual trespass of another life on the water.

I followed Karl, the stranger, watched him sit by the river, close to the sign advertising God. 'What shall it profit a man; if he shall gain the whole world, and lose his own soul?'

An elm tree sprayed with life in a field. A young man sat on the grass by the river. The Elizabethan fortress shoul-dered ivy.

Karl spoke little and when he did it was in the evening, in the pub, to the drovers. He was 'The Yank', but people tolerated this in him. He had no big car, no fast money, an urgency in his quietness, a distinction in his brows.

Margaret and Mona accustomed themselves to him and brought him to the bog with them. On an old ass and cart. Two young ladies with pitch forks in the bog, bottles of orange juice readily available, plastic bags of ice, and the summer sun at its height above them, grazing their work with its heat, its passing shadows, its sweltering fog towards evening. He helped them, becoming tanned; the complexion of sand on him, in his face, above his eyes, in his hair. He worked hard and silently. The ass wandered by the river and the girls frequently assessed the situation, sit-ting, drinking orange.

Margaret was the youngest but looked older; tall, pin-ched, cheek bones like forks on her and eyes that shot out, often venomously, often of an accord of their own, chestnut eyes that flashed and darted about and told an uncertain tale.

Mona was softer, younger-looking, mouse hair on her, a bush of it, and eyes that were at once angelic and reason-able. Her eyes told no tales though.

21

The river running through the bog was a savage one, foraging and digging, a merciless river that took sharp corners. Donkeys lazed by it; cows explored it; reeds shot up in it; in summer a silver glow on it that seduced.

Margaret and Mona were tolerant of me, using me to do messages, paying me with goldgrain biscuits or pennies. I talked to them though they didn't listen. They made a lot of cakes now and I sat licking bowls. Karl received their attention with moderate ease. He was slightly afraid of it yet glad of their kindness.

I felt him to be gentle though I wouldn't go so far as to say he hadn't done terrible things; however, what was more than likely was that he was haunted by the deeds of others.

In mid-July an American aunt came and visited Margaret and Mona, a lady from Chicago. She was from Karl's city and Karl visibly recoiled, going out more, seeking bog and river. This lady danced around, trimmed her eyebrows a lot, polished her nails.

She kept the girls in abeyance, talked to them as though talking to pet dogs. She had a blue hat that leapt up with a start, a slight veil hanging from the hat. She challenged everyone, me included, as to who they were, where they were from, who their parents were and what their ambition in life was. Karl was unforthcoming. I told her I was going to be a fire brigade man in China, but Karl said nothing, pulled on a cigarette, his eyes lifting a little.

She wanted to know where in Chicago he hailed from. He muttered something and she chattered on again, encompassing many subjects in her discursiveness, talking about the weather, the bog, her relatives in Armagh, Chicago, the Great Lakes, golf, swimming, croquet, timber forests, Indian reservations, the Queen, Prince Philip and lastly her dog, who'd jumped under a car one day when he'd been feeling – understandably – despairing.

Karl looked at though he was about to go when she left. The girls moved closer then, tried to ruffle him a bit, demanded more of him. He sang songs for them, recited poetry about American Indians. They listened. Mona had a song or two, songs about death and the banshee's call to death. Margaret was jealous of Mona's voice and showed her jealousy by pursing her scarlet lips.

They had parties again, entertaining the roguish young clerks. They had dances and sing-songs, the gramophone searing the nights with Ginger Rogers.

Karl went to church with them sometimes. He looked at the ceremonies as though at something difficult to understand, the hurried Latin, the sermons by the priest always muttered so low no one could hear them.

Mona went to Dublin early in September and bought new clothes. Margaret followed her example in doing this.

I went into the sitting room one evening and Margaret had her arm on Karl's shoulder. He talked about the war now for the first time, the planes, the screams, trees and houses fighting for their lives, the children moaning and the women grabbing their children. He recalled the fighter planes, the village targets; he spoke of the mercilessness of war. People asked for alms. They got war. Margaret recounted her father's tales about the Black and Tans, the butcheries, the maiming, and Mona philosophically added, 'Thank God we didn't have Churchill or Hitler here. Those men were just interested in the money.'

Margaret chirped in: 'About time someone got interested in money. They're starving beyond in England and Germany for want of money. We're lucky here.'

Ireland was the land of full and plenty to them, legends about other countries somehow awry.

Margaret boldly got up, put on the gramophone while I was there one evening and asked Karl to dance. Whereupon he threw off his shoes and danced with her, a waltz, the kernel of the music binding them together.

Mona watched, quiet, but not too jealous. They'd always been strange together and now the strangeness emerged. They saw in Karl a common ideal. They wanted to get him come hell or high water. High water came with the floods in early October. Mona outshone herself, russet in her hair, a dress of lilac and her arms brown from summer. Margaret became pertinent to the fact that Mona was more attractive than she, so she did many things, wore necklaces of pearl, daubed her lips in many colours, wore even higher high heels. She stood above Mona and was nearly as tall as Karl.

Their house had a bad reputation and now Margaret began appearing like an expensive courtesan; she wore her grandmother's fur to the pictures while all the time Mona shone with the grace of a Michaelmas daisy.

Geese clanked over; bare trees were reflected in water. The sun was still warm, the vibrancy and health of honey in it. The leaves had fallen prematurely and the floods had arrived before their time but still the days were warm and Mona wore sandals while Karl sported light jackets.

The ladies of town noted the combat between the two girls, or rather Margaret's unusual assertiveness. They were overjoyed and sensed a coming downfall on a house which had distressed them so much with its joyful sounds.

Karl had taken to talking to me, talking about Korea, Chicago, war, the race problem. He found a unique audience in me and I listened to everything and I watched his silences, his playing cards by himself. I started accompanying him on his walks; he sometimes sitting to read Chinese poems out loud while cows mooed appreciatively.

He took my hand once or twice and distilled in me the sense of a father. I suppose with Karl holding my hand then I decided I would have a child of my own some day, a male child.

Karl spoke, spoke of the weather in Chicago, winter storms over the Great Lakes, ice skating, swimming in the huge oblong winter pools. There was something Chicago didn't yield him, though, despite multi-layered ice-creams or skyscrapers always disappearing into the clouds, and that was the sky of Ireland, clouds over the mustard-coloured marshes, Atlantic clouds heaving and blowing and provoking rancour in the bog water. He'd come to our town looking for the ease of an Eastern shrine, found it. Now two young women were vying for him.

He spoke about his mother, his father, Americans, scoffed at the American belief in war. I told my parents that Karl didn't believe in war and they didn't hear me. I told my grandfather. Eventually I told our dog.

To the women of town Margaret and Mona were as courtesans, they'd stopped going to mass. God knows what they were doing with that American.

They made cakes, desserts, cups of tea for him. Eventually he tired of their intricacies and reached for them. One evening I came in the front door, pulled back the curtain to see Karl with Mona in his arms, her dress at her waist, her breasts heaving in her bra. I sped off.

I returned some evenings later, peeping through the curtains to find Margaret in a similar position.

Then one evening I came and the lights were off except for one red bulb that Karl had inserted. He and Mona were dancing to music from the radio in semi-darkness, the fire splurting and a rose light overlooking them, holding them.

This time I waited. I watched through the curtains as they danced, Karl reaching to kiss Mona. Their kiss was tantalizing. He removed her ribbon. Hair shot out like a hedgehog's prickles.

I knew Margaret to be in Dublin. I watched them leave the room. He followed her. I looked at Our Lady on an altar and she looked back at me quizzically. Outside a cat protested.

I don't know what happened that evening. I always imagine Margaret returned prematurely from Dublin and found them sleeping. But Karl left without saying goodbye and of all hurts I've had in my life that remains the most instant, the first hurt of life. My father, brother, friend, didn't acknowledge that a farewell was necessary.

It doesn't seem like a major incident looking back, but it took the rainbow from the girls' eyes, the flush from their cheeks, the splendour from their dress. Jealousy created a barrier. It created an iron curtain. Jealousy came and sat where Karl had once sat. Jealousy came, another tenuous stranger.

He was a celibate and didn't wish to make love to either but took Mona as an off-chance and showed to Margaret all that was missing in her: real physical beauty, a good singing voice.

Mona under the weight of Margaret's acrimony became plump, looked like an orphan in the convent.

No more parties, no more songs; many guests, much work.

And then in spring Mona left on the evening train. I went to the station with Margaret to say goodbye to her. Margaret looked like a lizard, fretful. Mona was wrapped like a Hungarian refugee. The sisters didn't kiss but I can still see the look in Mona's eyes. She'd been betrayed by Margaret's loss of faith in her. She undid her own beauty, the beauty of her soul as well as the beauty of her body to satisfy an impatient sister.

Years later when Mona was dying of cancer in a Birmingham hospital Margaret visited her. There was still no forgiveness, but both of them had forgotten what it was exactly which had come between them; a burgeoning of possibilities in the form of a young ex-soldier, an eye to another world. I doubt if either of them ever for a moment reached that other world but they were left with an intuition of it long after their father's money had run out.

Mona died a few years ago.

Margaret still runs the guest-house. And me? – I put these elements together to indicate their existence, that of Margaret and Mona, their enchantment with a young man who came and unnerved us all and left a strange aftermath, way back there in childhood, a shadow on the water, the cry of a wild goose in pain, an image of tranquillity in far-off Asia where candles burned before perennial gods, gods untouched by war, by the search of a young man, by the iniquitous failure of two young women who reached and whose fingers failed to grasp.

Afternoon

She lay in the hospital which she hated with nuns running about and nurses slipping with trays of soup.

The soup was awful, simply awful. 'Package soup,' she complained to Mary. Not the strong emerald and potato soup of the bog-roads. 'I'll die if I stay here much longer.' Mary looked at her. Her mother was ninety-one and the doctors had stated there was little hope for her. The tribe of the Wards was expecting death as their children would watch for the awakening of stars at night on beaches in Connemara.

Two Madges came and two more Marys came to see her later that night. They stood like bereaved angels gazing at the old woman who had mothered fifteen children, ten living, one a doctor in London, one a building contractor in California. The one who was a doctor had been taken by English tourists before the civil war. He'd been a blond two-year-old, her youngest at the time. They'd driven up in a Ford coupé to the camp, admired the child, asked if he could spend the summer with them. They never gave him back. Jimmy Joe was a building contractor in California. He'd gone to the golden state in 1925, seeking gold. He now owned a big house in San Francisco and Tim, her great-grandson, had only that summer gone to him and installed himself in the house, 'jumping into a swimming-pool' it was whispered.

Eileen lay dying. As the news spread Wards and even McDonaghs came to see her. They came with cloaks and blankets and children. They came with caps and with fine hats from London. They smoked pipes. They looked on with glazed eyes telling themselves about history of which she had seen so much.

Mary recalled the wake for her husband twenty years before in the fair green in Ballinasloe, loud mourning and the smell of extinguished fires. In the fair green of Ballinasloe now bumpers bashed and lights flashed to the sound of music and the rising whine of voices and machines.

Tinkers from all over Ireland had come to Ballinasloe fair green as they had for hundreds of years, bringing horses, donkeys, mules. Romanies even came from England and gipsies from the South of France.

Eileen in her hospital bed often thought she heard the voice of the carnvial. She'd first gone to the fair at the age of ten in 1895 when Parnell was still being mourned as this area was the place of his infamous adultery, adultery among the wet roses and the big houses of Loughrea. You could smell his sin then and the wetness of his sex. Her parents made love in their small caravan. In Ballinasloe there'd been the smell of horse manure rising balefully and the rough scent of limestone. A young man had asked her age and said she'd make a fine widow some day.

She'd married at fifteen and her husband went to sea. He sailed to South America and to South Africa and the last that was heard of him was that he'd married a black woman on an island.

Eileen had had one child by him. The child died in the winter of 1902 on a bog-road outside Ballinasloe. It had been buried in a field under the mocking voices of jackdaws and she swore she'd become a nun like the Sisters of Mercy in their shaded gardens in Ballinasloe.

But Joe Ward took her fancy – he'd become a tinker king in a fight in Aughrim – beating the previous king of the tinkers, who was twenty-five years older than him, in fist-fight. He'd been handsome and swarthy and had a moustache like British Army officers, well-designed and falling like a fountain.

They'd wedded in Saint Michael's church on Saint

Stephen's Day, 1906. Her father had told the bishop in Loughrea her previous husband had been eaten by sharks and the marriage had taken place without bother. She'd worn a Victorian dress, long and white, which the lady of the local manor had given her, a woman who'd performed on the London stage once with bouquets of paper roses about her breasts.

The priest had proclaimed them man and wife as celebrations followed on the Aughrim road, whiskey and poteen downed where a month before two children had died from the winter chill.

There had been dancing through the night and more than one young girl lay down with an older heftier man, and Eileen slept with a warm-legged man, forgetting about the odd clinging piece of snow and the geese fretting in the fields.

She became pregnant that cold, cold winter, holding her tummy as March winds howled and their caravans went west, trundling along Connemara roads to the gaps where the sea waited like a table. They camped near Leenane Head. Fires blazed on June nights as wails rose, dancing ensuing and wood blazing and crackling with a fury of bacon. They were good days. They'd sold a troop of white horses to the gipsies of France and many men went to bed with their women, stout in their mouths and on their whiskers.

They saw ships sail up the fjord at dawn and they bought crabs and lobster from local fishing men. When her belly had pushed out like a pram she found Joe on the lithe body of a young cousin.

Her child perished at birth. She had thirteen children by Joe. They grew up as guns sounded and tinker caravans were caught in ambushes in East Galway. Joe was in Dublin for 1916. He saw the city blaze and he was bitterly disappointed as he'd come to Dublin to sell a mare and eat a peach melba in an illustrious ice-cream house in Sackville Street. He returned to Galway without having eaten his ice-cream.

Michael Pat, her oldest, found a dead parish priest lying in the bushes like a crow in 1921; the Tans had smitten him on the head. The tinkers had covered his body and fallen on their knees in prayer. The police came and a long stalwart ambulance.

The body was borne away and Eileen and her children attended his funeral, bringing bouquets of daffodils stolen from the garden of a solicitor and banners of furze which were breaking to gold.

He was the last victim Eileen knew of, for Britain gave the men with their long moustaches and grey lichen-like hair their demands and as they arrived in Ballinasloe for the fair there was more anger, more shots, and buildings in flame in Dublin.

Irishmen were fighting Irishmen. A young man was led blindfold to a hill above the Suck and shot at dawn and the fair ceased for a day because of him and then went on with a girl who had a fruity Cork accent bellowing 'I'm forever blowing bubbles' across the fair green where lank and dark-haired gipsies from France smoked long pipes like Indians.

Eileen opened her eyes.

Her daughter Mary, sixty-two, looked like Our Lady of the Sorrows.

'O Mother dear you're leaving me alone with a pack of ungrateful children and their unfortunate and ill-behaved children.'

Mary was referring to her drunken sons and daughters who hugged large bottles of Jameson in Dublin with money supplied by social security or American tourists.

'Sure they have picnics of whiskey outside the Shelbourne,' Mary had once told her mother.

As for their children they were teddy boys and thieves and drunkards and swindlers or successful merchants of material stolen from bomb sites in Belfast. There was a group who went North in vans and waited like Apaches swooping upon bomb sites after the IRA had blown a store or a factory.

It was whispered that the IRA and the Irish tinkers were in league, blowing the Unionist kingdom to pieces for the betterment of the travelling people and for the ultimate ruinous joy of a dishevelled and broken province. Middle-aged men sat in parlours in Belfast thanking God for each exquisite joy of destruction, a bomb, a bullet, while they drank to the day there'd be a picture of Patrick Pearse in Stormont and a shoal of shamrocks on the head of Queen Victoria's statue. 'It's a bad picture of the travelling people folk have,' Mary had told her. And yet more and more were becoming peaceable and settling in council houses in Swinford or Castlerea. These were the ones you didn't hear of. These children who attended school and were educated and those parents who worked and who tidied a new house of slate grey. 'They say Tommy Joe is in the IRA,' Mary had said. Tommy Joe was Eileen's fifth great-grandson. Apparently he wore roses in his lapel and turned up in distant places, meeting agents or big-breasted young women, negotiating deals of arms. He ran off to Libya at the age of seventeen with an Irish melodion player who was a secret agent for a Belfast regiment.

That started him. 'It's been gin and tonic and sub-machine-guns since,' Mary had complained to Eileen before illness had confined her to Portiuncula Hospital, Ballinasloe.

As Eileen lay in bed surrounded by bustling sea-gull-like sisters from South America news filtered through of violence in the fair green.

It was the first year there'd been trouble at the fair other than brawls and fights and lusts. Men had been beaten with bottles. A caravan had been set alight and an old man in the country had been tied in his bed and robbed by two seventeen-year-old tinkers.

Eileen grabbed her beads.

It was the North, the North of Ireland was finally sending its seeds of ill-content among the travelling people. Young men who'd been to Belfast had caught a disease. This disease had shaped greed, had shaped violence like a way of grabbing, a way of distrusting, a way of relinquishing all Eileen had borne with her through her life.

Talking to Mary now, she said, 'England brought me great luck.'

She and Joe had travelled the length and breadth of Ireland as mares grew thin and men looked like mummers. They'd settled outside Belfast, dwelling on a site beside a graveyard while Joe, being a man of intelligence and strength, found work in the shipping yard. She'd had eleven grandchildren then and they hung their clothes like decorations on the bushes as her sons sauntered about Antrim on white horses repairing tin objects. One of her granddaughters fell in love with a minister's son. Eileen like her grandmother. She followed him about and when he ignored her she tore off her blouse, laying her breasts naked and her nipples like wounds and threatened to throw herself into the Lagan.

Peader her grandson led her away. The girl cracked up, became babbling and mad and ever after that went off with an old tinker called Finnerty, telling fortunes from palms, staring into people's eyes in Ballinasloe or Loughrea, foretelling people of death or scaldings or bankruptcy.

In the winter of 1935 Joe was beaten up and a young child seized by an Antrim lady who wouldn't let him go for two days, saying he was a heathen.

The sky dropped snow like penance and the Wards moved off, wandering through Donegal, past the mass rocks and the hungry bays and the small cottages closed to them and the hills teeming with the shadow of snow. There was no work for them and Brigid her youngest died of tuberculosis and four grandchildren died and Peader and Liam took boats to America and were not heard of till they got to Boston and were not heard of again until 1955 when both were dead.

'It's like the famine again,' said Eileen, recalling days close to her birth when the banshee howled and young men and old men crawled to the poor-house in Ballinasloe like cripples, seeking goat's milk.

Wirelesses blared jazz music as doors closed on them and Eileen cursed the living and the dead as she passed bishops' residences and crucified Christs hanging like bunting outside towns.

Her mother and father had survived the famine but they

lived to report the dead bodies lying over the length and breadth of Ireland like rotten turnips. They'd reported how men had hanged their children in order to save them and how at the Giant's Causeway Furies had eaten a McDonagh as though he was a chicken. 'We'll leave this land,' she said to Joe. They tried to sell their mangy mares, succeeded in Athenry in selling them to an Englishman as thin as the mares and they took off.

'Our people have been travelling people since the time of St Patrick,' said Joe. 'We should have been treated better than this.'

Sister woke her.

'Wake up, Mrs McDonagh. It's time for breakfast.' She was not Mrs McDonagh but the nun presumed all tinkers were McDonaghs.

Breakfast was porridge thin and chill as the statue of Mary standing somewhere near.

Eileen ate as a young nurse came and assisted her as though shovelling earth into a grave.

'The tea is putrid,' complained Eileen.

'Whist,' said the nurse. 'You're only imagining it.'

Outside mists clung like a momentary hush. Winter was stealing in but first there was this October imminence, standing above sweetshops and council houses.

She took one more sup of the tea.

'This is not good enough.' She called the nurse. A country girl made off to get her stronger tea as Eileen bemoaned the passing of tea thick and black as bog-water.

They'd set up camp in Croydon in 1937, and from that spot moved across England, repairing tin, selling horses, rambling north along ill-chosen sea-side paths, paths too narrow for jaunty caravans. They surmounted this island, rearing right to its northmost edge, the Kyle of Lochalsh, John o' Groat's.

They camped in winter in mild spots where men shook herring from their nets as Eileen's daughters shook daughters and sons from their bodies, as the Wards germinated and begot and filled England with tinkers.

During the war they craved their little spot in Croydon, venturing north but once, shoeing horses in Northumberland, taking coast roads, watched by ancient island monasteries. They settled in Edinburgh winter of '42 but Eileen got lonesome for talk of Hitler and the air-raid shelters squeezing with people and she left a city of black fronts and blue doors and went south with Joe and her daughter Mary, widowed by a man who jumped into the sea to save a bullock from drowning.

They camped in Croydon. Mary married a cockney tramp and they broke Guinness into an old bath and feasted on it. Mary had three children and more people of their clan joined them.

At Christmas they had the previous year's trees fished from rubbish dumps and they sang of the roads of Ireland and ancient days, bombs falling as they caroused without milk or honey.

He didn't come back one day and she searched London three days and three nights, passing rubble and mothers bemoaning their dead children until his body was found in a mortuary. She didn't curse Hitler or his land. She fell on her knees and splayed prayers and lamentation over his dead body as further sirens warned of bombs, and, as her body shaking with grief became young and hallucinatory, imagining itself to be that of a girl in Connaught without problems.

They buried him in London. The McDonaghs and the Wards and the McLoughlins came and as it was winter there were only weeds to leave on his grave but the women shook with crying and the men pounded their breasts.

Above Eileen saw geese fly north.

She woke with tears in her eyes and she wiped them with hospital linen. 'Joe, Joe. My darling lover. Joe, Joe, where did you go, times when bombs were falling like bricks and little girls were lying in the rubble like china dolls.'

She was leading woman of her tribe then. Her family gathering, hanging their washings like decorations.

At Christmas 1944 a duchess drove up with presents for the

children. She had on a big hat of ermine grey and Eileen refused her gifts, knowing her kinsmen to have fought this aristocracy for nine hundred years and realizing she was being made a charity of. Once in Ballinasloe she'd known a lady who'd been a music hall artiste in London and who married the local lord. That lady had addressed her as her equal.

Eileen had had hair of purple and red then and she'd had no wish of charity. The lady of the house had found companionship in a girl living in a tent on the edge of her estate.

'We'll go back to Ireland,' her son Seamus said at the end of the war.

Eileen hesitated. She was not sure. The last memories had been mangy. She and her family were English-dwelling now and they received sustenance for work done and they abided with the contrasts of this country.

She led her family north before deciding. Up by Northumberland and seeing a fleet of British planes flying over she decided on embarking.

The customs man glared at her as though she was an Indian.

'Are you Irish, ma'am,' he said.

'Irish like yourself,' she said.

He looked at her retinue.

'Where were ye?' he said. 'In a concentration camp?'

They travelled straight to Galway. Its meadows still were sweet but on the way men had looked crossly at them and women suspiciously. This was the land her parents had travelled. It had not even a hint of the country beset by famine. Cars were roaming like hefty bullocks and in Athenry as they moved off from Ballinasloe little Josephine Shields was killed.

A guard came to look at the crash.

'I'm sorry,' he told Eileen. 'But you can't be hogging these roads. Something like this has been bound to happen.'

They buried the little girl in Galway. There was a field of daisies nearby and Eileen's eyes rose from the ceremony to the sea spray and a hill where small men with banana bellies were playing golf.

'I'm leaving this land,' she told herself.

They journeyed back to Liverpool, erupting again on the face of England, germinating children like gulls. They moved north, they moved south and in Croydon, standing still, Eileen met Joseph Finnerty, half-Irish tinker, half-French gipsy by his mother's origin. They married within two months. He was thirty-nine. She was sixty-two. She was a good-looking woman still and welcomed his loins. Their marriage was celebrated by a priest from Swaziland and performed in Croydon. Tinkers came from Ireland, more to 'gawp' said Eileen and gipsies, wild and lovely from France.

'My family has broken from me like a bough,' said Eileen. 'Now it's my turn for the crack.'

Men of ninety found themselves drunk as hogs in hedges about Croydon. A black priest ran among the crowd like a hunted hare and a young girl from Galway sang songs in Irish about deaths and snakes and nuns who fell in love with sailors.

Eileen looked at the London suburb as though at the sea.

'I can return to Ireland now,' she said.

She brought him back and they travelled widely, just the two of them for a while.

She brought him back to old spots, Galway and the Georgian house where the gentry lived and the girl from the London music hall of the last century. They went to the sea and marvelled at the way-side contrasts of furze and rhododendrons in May.

Joseph played a tin whistle and there was dancing along the way and singing and nights by high flames when a girl stepped out of Eileen like a ballerina.

'The years have slipped off your face,' people told her. They went to a dance one night in Athenry where there was jazz music and they danced like the couples with the big bellies and the bouncing hair.

'I'll take you to my mother's country now,' said Joseph, so off they went in a van that wheezed like a dying octogenarian through France.

They passed houses where they heard music the like Eileen could not understand, thrilling music, music of youth, music of a cosmos that had changed.

They passed war ruins and posters showing brazen women. They weaved through towns where summer lingered in February and rode hills where spring came like an onlooker, gazing at them with eyes of cherry blossom. They lingered on a mound of earth as they caught sight of a blue, blue sea.

They got out.

'This is my real home,' Joseph said. 'The Camargue. My mother's people came from here. This is the heart of the tinkers' world. I was born here, of a father from Kerry and a mother from Saintes Maries de la Mer. I was gifted with second sight and feet that moved so I spend my first days in Ireland and saw the fighting and the flags and the falling houses and then I came back here and danced the wild dances and loved the strong women. From Marseilles I went south.' He pointed. 'Over there is Egypt. I arrived there when I was twenty-six and from there my life flows. I recall the palm trees and the camels as though it was yesterday. I went there and understood, understood our people the world over, the travelling people, men who moved before Gods were spoken of, men who – who understood.'

'We are of an ancient stock, my father used to say,' said Eileen. 'We were here before St Patrick and will be when he's forgotten.'

'Our secrets are the secrets of the universe,' said Joseph, 'a child, a woman with child, a casual donkey. We are the sort that Joseph was when he fled with Mary.'

Sand blew into Eileen's eyes as she drank wine for the first time. In March she watched young men with long legs from Hungary ride into the sea with red flags. It was the feast of St Sarah, patron saint of gipsies.

They carried her statue like a bride betrothed to the sea and praised her with lecherous and lusty tongues.

The sea was already taking the shape of summer, a blue, blue sea.

'In October they come again to celebrate,' Joseph explained. 'They are faithful to their saints.'

She sat on sands where she drunk bottles of wine and bottles of Coca-Cola and walked by the sea which asked of her, 'Is this folly?'

She wanted to go home. She wished like a child fatigued of fun to see Ireland again.

'I'd like to take off soon,' she said to Joseph but she saw coming across his face a villainous look. He was drunk with red wine and wandering by the sea like an old man in Leenane. 'I want to go,' she told herself, 'I want to go.'

Summer edged in. She plucked wild flowers and wondered about her children and her children's children and asked herself if this her cup had not brimmed too high. 'Was it all folly?' she demanded of herself. Was it a madness that drove people littler than herself into Ballinasloe mental hospital to enquire daily if they were saints or sinners. She began to wonder at her own sanity and placed wine bottles full of wild roses on the sands of Carmargue before crying out, 'Am I going mad? Am I going mad?' They brought her first to a priest, then to a doctor in Marseilles. They left her alone in a white room for two days.

'Joseph Finnerty I curse you,' she said. Then he came and took her and placed her on a horse and rode towards their caravans in Camargue. 'We're going back to Ireland,' he said.

They arrived on a June morning and they set tracks to Connaught. The day was fine and on the way they heard that O'Rourke, king of the tinkers, was dead. 'You'll be the next king of the tinkers,' Eileen said.

She arranged he fight Crowley his opponent in Mountshannon. Women stood by with Guinness and cider and children paddled among the fresh roses and geraniums. She saw her lover strip to the waist and combat a man his senior and she recalled her father's words, 'Lucky is the man who wins ye.'

This man over the others had won her.

She wrapped a shawl about her as they fought and fell to

the ground. In the middle of combat her gaze veered from fight to lake where birds dropped like shadows. 'I have travelled at last,' she said. 'There's a hunger and a lightness returned to my body. A grandmother and mother I'm not no more but a woman.'

After Joseph fought and won they drove off to a pub pushing out from a clump of rhododendrons and celebrated.

'Jesus, Mother,' said Mary. 'Have you no sense?'

'Sense I haven't but I have a true man and a true friend,' she said.

She was held in high esteem now and where she went she was welcomed. Age was creeping up on her but there were ways of sidling away from it.

She'd jump on a horse and race with Joseph. He was a proud man and faithful to her.

Also he was a learned man and conversed with school teachers.

In Cairo he'd had tuition from French Jesuits. He spoke in French and English and Romany and could recite French poets or Latin poets.

When it came to his turn at a feast he'd not play the whistle but sing a song in the French language.

Finally he grew younger before her eyes as she grew older. In France she'd fled because it was a bad match. Here there was nowhere to go.

It was lovely, yes, but her eyes were becoming criss-crossed like potato patches.

'I have reached an age that leads towards the grave,' she wept to herself one evening, 'I am an old banshee.' Joseph comforted her, not hearing, but maybe knowing.

She watched him bathe in the Shannon and knew he should be with a woman younger than her but that yet she loved him and would cut her throat for him. She saw in his eyes as he looked from the water the stranger that he was and the stranger that he was going to be.

In 1957 he fell from a horse in the fair green in Ballinasloe and was killed.

39

She remembered the curse on him in the South of France and knew it to have come true.

She watched the flames burning and coaxing at the wake and recalled his words in France. 'Our secrets are the secrets of the universe, a child, a woman with child, a casual donkey. We are the sort that Joseph was when he fled with Mary.' He was educated by French Jesuits and held corners in his tongue and twists in his utterances. He was a poet and a tinker and a child of the earth.

She recalled the lady in the manor long ago who'd befriended her, to whom she'd go with bushels of heather on summer evenings.

Why was it that women had been haunting and troubling her mind recently.

It had been so long since she'd known her yet she bothered her. Had it been warning of Joseph's death. All her life despite the fact she was just a tinker she'd met strange people.

From the woman in the manor who'd asked her to tea one day, to the French gipsy who'd become her lover as old age dawned upon her. He'd been the strangest of all, brown face, eyes that twinkled like chestnuts in open pods. Yes, he'd been a poet as well as a lover. He'd been of the earth, he'd gone back to it now. He'd possessed the qualities of the unique like the cockney music-hall girl who'd attracted the attention of an Irish peer and came to live in a manor, finding a friend in a tinker from a hovel of tents and caravans.

She watched the flames dance and saw again the white horses of Camargue, flurrying in uncertain unison, and would have walked into the fire ablaze had someone not held her and comforted her and satiated her as her moans grew to the sound and shape of seals in bays west of Ballinasloe.

'Eileen wake up. Do you know what's happened. They've killed an old man.'

Eileen looked at her daughter. 'Who?'

'Tinker lads.'

Eileen stared. So death had come at last. They'd killed an old man. 'May they be cursed,' she said, 'for bringing bad tidings on our people. May they be forsaken for leaving an old way of life, for doing what no travelling people have ever done before.'

As it happened the old man was not dead. Just badly beaten up.

Some tinkers had gone to rob him, took all and hit him with a Delft hot-water jar.

'The travellers have already gone from the green.'

'Ballinasloe fair week without the tinkers,' Eileen said. 'What a terrible sight the green must be.'

She saw more tinkers than she'd ever seen before.

They came like apostles as a priest rummaged with broken words.

'Is it dying you think I am? Well, it's not dying I am,' said Eileen.

She saw five children like the seven dwarfs. 'These too will grow to drink cider outside the Gresham in Dublin,' she thought, as candles lit and the priest talked about the devil.

Her great-grandson Owen was living with a rich American woman in an empty hotel in Oughterard. 'What next?'

Her head sunk back.

She saw Joseph again and the flames and wanted again to enter but knew she couldn't. She woke.

'If it's dying I am I want to die in peace. Bring me to the crossroad in Aughrim.' A Pakistani doctor nearly had concussion but the solemn occasion speeded up as a nun intervened.

Young nurses watched Eileen being carted off.

They lay her on the ground and a Galway woman keened her. The voice was like sharp pincers in her ears.

Now that they were saying she was on the verge of death ancient memories were budging and a woman, the lady of the manor was moving again, a woman in white, standing by french windows, gazing into summer.

41

She'd had fuzzy blonde hair and maybe that was why she'd looked at Joseph more closely the first time she saw him. She had the same eyes, twinkling brazen eyes.

She heard again the lady's voice. 'No, I won't go in,' answering her husband. 'It's not evening. It's just the afternoon.'

Eileen woke.

The stars shone above like silver dishes. The bushes were tipped with first frost.

She stirred a bit. 'Is it better I'm getting?' she wondered. She moved again and laughed.

Her bones felt more free. She lifted her head. 'They might be killing old men but they won't kill me.'

She stirred. A girl heard her.

Women shook free from tents and gazed as though at Count Dracula.

In the morning she was hobbling on a stick.

She hobbled down the lane and gazed on the Galway road. 'I'll have duck for dinner,' she said. 'Ye can well afford it with all the shillings you're getting from the government.'

At Christmas she was able to hobble, albeit with the help of a stick into the church, crossing herself first with holy water.

Embassy

She ran a pub where old men slouched over Guinness and where the light was always dark. Two or three regular customers were always there and the conversations revolved around sick dogs or bottled ships as these were an important property in the community, symbolizing social status and a good clean home.

The calendar in the pub literally looked as though it was about to fester and give. A doll-like model was represented on it. She was leaning over a log and her lips were red.

She had blue eyes, delicately outlined by black. She wore a brown coat and despite the snow on distant pines she did not look at all cold.

Sheila would stand by the counter talking to all who came in, occasionally cleaning a glass, rubbing it with a cloth.

Her husband had left her five months now and her children were gone, married, working on the bogs in the midlands and she was alone.

But she was glad she was alone. The house was falling down. A brown faded photograph of a distant Edwardian relative stood askew on the stairway. Nettles brandished themselves in the garden, the odd Guinness bottle thrown among them, but she was happy. She went to bed at night with 'Sauce-pan', the big brown cat, on the eiderdown and she slept peacefully, dreaming of girlhood dances when she waltzed at the cross-roads, framed in a black dress with a topaz necklace on her white bosom.

She'd been a famous beauty then and even in the big house

43

with raging Virginia creeper beyond the canal there weren't girls to come near her in beauty.

She had a quality ministers' daughters or doctors' daughters, lawyers' daughters or senators' daughters couldn't rival. She had black hair wild and as crossed as blackberries and her skin was rich and olive. She had six sisters, none to come near her in beauty and as such she was marked out and her sins counted.

She'd dance at the crossroads with the doctor's sons and the lawyer's sons and often there'd be coloured lights nearby or a caravan with the lakes of Killarney painted on it as an excuse for a carnival.

Girls at the village molested her with stares but she didn't care and went to Mullingar with doctors' sons who had rich woollen jerseys and bright broad bones in a country where other men stood silently on streets, holes in their trousers and handkerchiefs trailing out of their pockets.

They were good old days to talk to her customers about and she didn't really care if they had not attended the dances. She didn't really care if no one else remembered the day Dr Dehilly's son pinched her cheeks and said they were the colour of scarlet. He had been the boy she mostly had her eye on. He had red check handkerchiefs spilling out of his pocket and he always looked at though he was about to swing a golf-club, alert, agile. He took her five times to a dance in Mullingar and once to dinner in Dublin.

When she came back he stopped seeing her and she had the ire and jealousy of local girls to deal with. But she didn't care. Her own sisters were cruel and cutting, and to make things worse she'd been jilted by him, but she raised her head and kept it high and if they breathed bad words about her hadn't she had his good looks and his smile for five weeks and the pleasure of his company in Dolphin's Hotel in Dublin?

Her clothes were cheap and often second-hand which caused scandal to her family but it had to be admitted at a dance she looked better than most refined of the young, a

'French painter's model' someone said. She had good taste and if she had the looks sure she might as well make use of them.

It was going too far, however, when she started roaming the fields in summer with farmers' sons. The streets of the village were bare and deserted, the canal usually low on water and if there weren't poppies in the fields there'd be no colours other than green of grass or gold of hay.

What she did in the fields with those young men no one knew but one rather mad young man gave her a mother of pearl bead owned by his grandmother and another said afterwards she was as fine to be with as a whore in Dublin. She didn't care. She raised her head higher and walked the one main carniverous street of the village, waiting to be chastised, knowing she never would be openly, defiant if you like, brave.

There was a priest at the time with a rhubarb neck whom people said the African sun had made somewhat crazy and he hollered each Sunday as money rattled.

He collected money at funerals and weddings and it would almost make you cry to see the bereaved at a funeral give their silver to a little lizard of a man who with the priest was like the local mafiosi.

This priest hollered one Sunday about Jezebels and daughters of Satan, and Sheila felt like standing, ordering her stance and making a speech in favour of sin. She'd discovered sin to be warm and vibrant and thoroughly to be recommended.

That was in the bad old days. Now Ireland had changed and her nieces courted men on the pavement outside and priests talked about sex and the papers wrote about it. Behind her counter Sheila felt glad that somewhere she'd inaugurated it and laughed at the dreary dirty jokes of her customers.

Five months before her husband had left her. Her husband used to run the pub with her and read Joyce's *Portrait of the Artist as a Young Man* over the counter but then he tired of her fits and got the mail boat from Holyhead and went away.

Sheila's fits were known to all her family. She'd threaten to burn the house down or kill herself, or she'd stand on the stairway at night shouting abuse at her son. No one knew why she did it.

She was the black sheep of the family, always isolated, always blamed and as such into middle age she felt she ought to drag an element of nuisance.

She tried to choke her husband one night, not seriously, but in a fit of anger with herself alighted on him. He stared back. Once he'd loved her. But as she'd grown older she'd made such a nuisance of herself that he tired of her.

He backed a lot of horses. He drank a lot of Guinness.

She'd call him names if he spilt porter on the floor; make him clean it up. As her daughter grew up she grew jealous of her and gave her a difficult time. As her son grew up she was more relaxed but often lost her temper with him and boxed him in the ears. Then she was sorry. But it was too late.

They tried to put her in a mental hospital many times but she refused to go. She knew her rights and lay them on the table. People stared at her exasperated, but that didn't bother her. There was something more she wanted to know about.

She'd go into the garden and recognize the supreme quality of untidiness there and ask herself why she hadn't tended a garden like the local lawyer's or the Protestant minister's with its orange undercurrent blaze of nasturtiums in autumn or its bed of baby raspberries in summer.

What was wrong with her inheritance?

She took a broom one night and set it alight; after that her husband left her. He got a job in Shepherd's Bush in London and lived with two young labourers.

'Driven from house and home,' people said. He returned two months later for his daughter's wedding when there were pound notes stuck about the house and when people danced at the crossroads again. The pub wasn't doing too well so she borrowed clothes from her sister in Ballinasloe and she danced at the wedding, regardless.

'I know what they're saying,' she thought. 'They're saying I'm odd and queer. I have a hat the wrong way round and my shoes are too big for me. That doesn't stop me from dancing, does it?'

Her son went to work in Bord na Mona, the Irish peat company, and one evening in the pub she read that they'd found an ancient Irish crozier in the bog where he worked. 'Wonders never cease,' she told an old man dormant on her counter. He didn't reply. She poured herself a bottle of Guinness and toasted her children, her daughter married to a rich garage owner, her son living in a flat in a town in the Western Midlands with a jukebox in the restaurant below him.

'He'll be listening to Elvis tonight,' she thought, recalling Elvis's latest song 'In the Ghetto'.

Things went from bad to worse. People stopped going to her pub altogether and she hardly had sixpence.

No wonder she tried to burn the house down one day. That was it. She was carted off to the hospital in Mullingar. She wondered what she'd done wrong or why it was she was always doing things people didn't favour, like driving her husband away or boxing her daughter's ears or burning her house down. 'There must be something wrong with me,' she thought, yet she resented being the troublesome one of the family. That made her worse. It made her more war-like.

Yet how could she have told anyone how happy she'd been in that house which was falling apart. She'd seen a total of nine mice in it, thought she heard a rat, but alone, left in her ways she cut an edge on happiness.

Then one night she had a nightmare in which her dead mother chased her downstairs and Sheila rose and systematically tried to burn the house to the ground.

'Why did you do it?' her sister from Ballinasloe asked and she could only answer 'I got bored.'

Sheila had a retinue of faithful relatives, she provided a focus for their misgivings on life and also a centre point about which they could talk of their endless problems.

Sheila was the biggest problem of all. Yet no one had noticed she'd been happy in her second-hand clothes at her daughter's wedding.

47

The mental hospital didn't suit her. 'All of them queer people,' she told her sister. 'Can't I get out of here?'

By a stroke of luck a job was secured for her in an embassy in Dublin. They packed her off with good clean clothes and she took up the post of char-lady in a big mansion off Ailesbury Road. She had a little room to herself and was fascinated to see a row of red-brick houses when she woke in the morning instead of trees and grass wasted by bad earth.

She rose at early hours and did her chores, bringing tea to the ambassador and his workers.

She cleaned carpets scrupulously and sometimes stopped to look at portraits of Scandinavian dignitaries or oil paintings of Irish scenes by leading Irish artists.

In her village there'd been an artist among their flock of maidens, but the girl had been so cantankerous that it might have put you off art for life. Looking at these pictures now Sheila felt a blue day dawning in her. Gone were her memories of her children's adolescence and her husband's exasperation with her. She felt a lightness in her womb, like a birth.

Here they had honey on their toast in the mornings and they served wine with lunch.

She loved it. If she'd had a close female friend she'd have written to her all about it but as she'd had none she kept silent. Her husband now seemed like a stranger and her children, always angry with her, would never understand.

But there was a unique growth which she herself understood and wanted to describe but there was no one to tell about it so she became devout, praying, because at least God could hear and know that one was grateful.

Croissants were brown and crispy in the mornings and serving them she hummed the only song she knew of 'Non, je ne regrette rien'. The ambassador liked her cheerful face and seeing herself in the mirror she wondered why she hadn't smiled more often.

It was proper to have a happy face and then she remembered her lineage, her birth into a dour family and wondered at what chance she could have had. But replacing that understanding was a clean new emotion, there was a beginning which was eroding the past and its lack of peace. She was beginning again.

As her wages were high she found herself buying new clothes and picking up lace and delicate things. She bought herself a ring with Connemara marble at the centre of it and often admired it on her finger as she dusted a carpet. It symbolized all growth in her. She went to a window and looked out and instead of one magpie as she'd seen on her wedding day there were two. 'One for sorrow, two for joy.' She remembered chanting that on her way from the church with her husband. He was in England now. He'd been working as a foreman in his pea-factory. She'd driven him away, yet why worry she told herself. She remembered his skinny body in his pyjamas in bed and she rejoiced she was here in Dublin, away from home and family. She arrested an insect in his march across the wainscot and shook him into the air.

A delegation of dignitaries passed her. She rose. They smiled at her. She continued work.

A man who worked as secretary in the embassy smiled at her more than anybody else and one morning when she was having coffee he approached her and offered her a cigarette. He had thick blond hair, though he was about fifty, and he had a large handsome smile. He enquired her name of her and she told him. He seemed pleased. He introduced himself as Dag. They smoked cigarettes and gently he eased information from her about her environment. He'd worked in the United Nations. He liked Dublin, he said, liked the Irish. He was interested in this country.

She acted like a child under surveillance. He left her but later in the afternoon, cleaning the waiting-room he came behind her and indicated a painting. 'Carl Larsson,' he said. 'A Swedish painter.'

The painting showed children feasting in a summer scene with a bottle thrown amid the grass. 'That is how it was,' he said, 'when I was a child.'

Sheila looked at him. He seemed odd and beautiful. Maybe he was lonesome for home.

He talked to her often after that. She didn't know why. He talked of the city whence he came, rivers running through it, water-reeds growing, church towers dark and threatening and rain, rain always falling. A biscuit snapped in Sheila's teeth.

'You like it here better?' she asked.

'It's fun,' he said simply.

She wondered why he approached her so much. Would she become coquettish, she wondered.

She stared at a box of marigolds outside a window one day. What was it that led her here she wondered, was it the force of salvation itself. Her thoughts came easier. A stranger was making conversation with her and she was glad, glad of words, talk, coffee to accompany them.

He told her about trees in his city which they tried to cut down but which the people did not allow. He told her about a poet who stayed in the trees in a hammock. He described how they still stood, green and bold in summer and how the young ate strawberries under them. Sheila thought of her own young and a wisp of guilt flew through her.

He was a kindly person. He liked books. He talked of the Town Hall in his city where great men had been honoured by the Nobel prize. Sheila looked at him and said, 'Isn't it a funny thing how men reach their goals?' He smiled at that remark and said it was beautiful.

'Would you like to join me for dinner tomorrow?' he asked.

Sheila was delighted. 'Where?' she asked. He suggested the Shelbourne.

She met him there and he fondled her warm hands as though they were gloves and they ate veal. She didn't want wine. It was too much of a luxury. He talked again of his home country, mentioning the far lands up north where snow fell and the sun never set in summer, where the Laps wandered, a people clothed in deer-skin with caps, and eyes staring from caps – like moles.

It was the country of his youth, he said, everyone has a country of their youth.

Sheila considered her own home town and regretted so much those moments that there had been no such place in her youth but was comforted when he talked of children dying in Asia. Other people had their problems too.

She said goodbye to him at the top of Grafton Street and felt ridiculous and left, going back to work. Staring at the Larsson picture she noticed odd things about the figures and would have asked the artist to correct them if he'd been about.

She met him again the following morning as he smiled but he didn't stop to talk to her.

He was busy. She saw him having coffee with some diplomats and was glad he didn't talk to her because she understood his work to be more important than her. She dusted oak and pinewood and was glad of its sweet smell, near her nose as she bent to dust it.

There was one room in the embassy where there was a chink of stained glass and Sheila went there, in awe of it. She loved its particularity and one day she was standing there when he put his arm on her shoulder. She laughed.

He laughed. He sat and asked her what it was about Irishwomen and she said she didn't know and he spoke about his dead wife, Elizabeth, and he cried.

She gave him her new clean handkerchief and he said more than anything he wanted children but his wife had had no children.

'There were alderberries around our summer home,' he said. 'I always wanted to share their taste with children.'

She put her arm about him and he held her, quite platonically and then he let go of her and apologized. His wife was beautiful he said. They didn't get on.

And he intimated darker things about her death.

Sheila was living in a world miles from the one she used to inhabit. She rose in the mornings, serene, calm and dressed herself neatly. She understood herself to be miles beyond

EMBASSY

pain and thought they would never reach her here, they
being relatives and the mangy dogs of her village.

She went about her chores and each day took time off to
talk to her new friend, not about the problems of the third
world which he knew so much about but the areas of pain,
loss that the human being encounters.

He whispered things about his home country, about
wheaten-coloured grass and boats on the Archipelago and
she in turn thought of golf-playing doctors in the hungry
fields about her home.

He took her one day in the pantry and kissed her. She
walked about for two days, understanding this kiss, knowing
it was not from passion it was given but from appreciation.

Her sister wrote to her and asked her how she was getting
on. She didn't reply.

Her friend asked her to dinner and she turned up in a new
turtle brown suit. They had white wine and now she laughed
more freely and her eyes were becoming wider.

They were in Wynn's hotel which caters for priests and
nuns. Suddenly over a table she saw her sister. Her sister
looked at her, half from embarrassment. Sheila jumped up
and introduced her friend. Her sister smiled a sad knowledgeable smile and left.

They left her alone for three weeks and then began writing
suddenly, asking her how she was.

They hadn't written before, her husband, son, daughter,
sister but suddenly a barrage of letters came.

She didn't reply to any of them. She had a picture by Carl
Larsson in her room and the plant on the window she
watered carefully.

In August her friend told her he had to go back to his
country on urgent business. She said goodbye to him as if he
was only going for a few days and walked about the town
where French students were thronging. It was there she met
her sister again. Her sister recognized her happiness and her
ability to cope and smiled.

They went to a café and had tea.

Her sister asked her questions about work but Sheila could not reply the way she would have done once, she knew other things now and the things she knew about did not make her despair.

Her friend did not come back and she went to the zoo and looked at the polar bears and thought of him. She shopped for herself and at Christmas bought perfumes for her daughter and sister. But still there was no word about him.

She went to mass on Christmas morning in the Carmelite church off Grafton Street and shared Christmas with the charwoman.

Her husband wrote from London. She never finished his letter. Her daughter and son sent customary greetings. Her sister wrote a short note.

In the new year when he didn't come and when it snowed she felt an august closeness to him, crossing the green, partial to light and golden shadow. She knew that in his country the earth would be covered like this. She wanted to write to him but didn't have his address, all she desired to do was to register this complicity again.

The mornings were clean and blue and she looked at the sky when she rose and realized now she was happier than ever.

Her sister sent her some clothes and her husband asked her about separation. Her daughter wrote an abusive letter to her, just suddenly out of the blue, accusing her of cruelly ruining her adolescence. Sheila put the letter from her but she realized somewhere she was crying inside. Yes, she had been bad.

She crossed streets now by herself and sometimes found herself crying in a café. She drank tea, looking about suspiciously, fearful of someone alien to her entering.

At night she began having nightmares. These nightmares disturbed her suddenly. They were like someone with a red hot poker. She'd rise, almost as though there was a substance present. She'd reach out but there'd be no one there and she'd go back to sleep, dreaming of the canal at home and the houses staring like spinsters.

Sometimes over work she'd break down crying.

53

These times were noted with compassion and a doctor was brought. The doctor gave her pills but then one day her daughter arrived, hatred in her eyes, telling her maybe she should have a 'rest'. She knew what they meant.

She allowed them to lead her as though in trance wishing punishment for all her sins.

After three weeks it was understood there was nothing wrong with her so she left the mental hospital but her job had been filled and she had to go back to her house.

She reopened her pub. The old faces returned like dreary dogs. She sat in the pub and sometimes didn't move but waited, waited as though for fate to punish her.

It didn't come and she spent three months like this.

Her relatives checked her but found she was not creating fits. Her husband obtained a legal separation from her. Her children never wrote.

She knew the wrong she was doing herself and often thought to leave but something kept her here, the weight of the past, the time she boxed her daughter's ears, the time she hit her son with a brush.

Flame burned in front of the Sacred Heart. There was no piety for such a figure in her heart.

She went about her work. She fed her cats.

One day, however, she did go to Dublin. She got a train from Mullingar.

She had a handbag under her arm. She had a brown hat with a velvet ribbon on. She wore a grey suit.

It was like going back to a dream, a dream not tested before, an interim in her life when all made sense.

She walked up Grafton Street and nearing the top she had a heart-attack.

It was outside a bookshop and a priest tended to her and her people were both glad and shocked. They were glad she was dead but shocked at the suddenness of her finish. But none of them knew the secret she shared with a diplomat miles from this place.

Approaching the green she saw that the trees were in

bloom and she observed that the leaves were pushing through the railings. She thought of a city faraway where trees were saved from being destroyed by the response of the people and she knew that because they stood, those trees, something was alive that neither her death, nor the death of others, her sadness, nor the sadness of others, could destroy. They buried her without much ceremony.

Her daughter wept. Her son stood as though paralysed.

The figures walked away.

One figure stood alone, that of her daughter, her ears still ringing with the memory of a punch from her mother long ago.

But the occasion moved her to wait.

She walked away minutes later. They sold her house, the cats were sent to a cats' home and people ultimately were relieved.

It was as though by closing her off they were putting a seal forever on all of life's misfortunes.

A Poet and an Englishman

'We'll shortly see the broad beaches of Kerry,' he said, smiling, the van ricketing from side to side and Limerick's fields passing, pastures of golden, or near golden, dandelions.

His hair swung flamingly over his face, a wild red gust of hair and his tinker's face narrowed like a gawky hen's.

'Peader.' She swept her hand across his forehead and he laughed.

'Behold the Golden Vale.'

They got out and looked. Sandra's legs were white after winter, white as goat-skin. A sort of vulnerable white Peader thought.

Her body was tucked into a copper dress and her hair, red like his, performed little waves upon her shoulders. She looked so handsome. After a winter in Belfast that was strange. One would have thought a winter in Belfast would have changed one, broken-down factories and hills, arching with graves.

Yet in their little house off Springfield Road, they'd hid out, guns going off occasionally, televisions roaring, an odd woman calling.

Peader was working as a tradesman-carpenter-cum-electrician. A strange trade for a tinker one might have thought. Peader had picked these skills up in London when he ran away from Michael Gillespie, his tutor, in the west of Ireland.

He was seventeen and his hair was more gold than red and he'd run away from the harbour village where he'd been brought up and partly adopted by an English Greek teacher who'd retired to Ireland on the strength of a volume of poems, a hard-bitten picturesque face in *The Times* colour supplement and an award from the British Arts Council.

There in the west he stayed, making baskets, sometimes taking to the sea in a small boat, writing more poems, winning more awards, giving lectures in Greek to students at Irish colleges.

Peader thought of Michael now, thought of him because somehow the words framed in his head were the sort of words Michael would use.

'A sort of vulnerable white.' Yes, that was the state of Sandra's legs; they were pale and cold. Ready for summer.

'Let's make love,' Peader thought in his head and he didn't need to say it to Sandra. There were bushes and leaving their van there on the open road above the Golden Vale, they hid behind bushes where Sandra could have sworn there was honeysuckle just about to appear and made love, Peader coming off in her, rising like a child caught in an evil but totally satisfying act.

'Banna Strand.' Peader murmured the name of the beach. Roger Casement had appeared on that beach in a German submarine in 1916 and was arrested and hanged.

'Our first sight of the sea,' Sandra said.

'It's lovely.'

It stretched, naked, cold.

'I'd love a swim,' Sandra thought, thinking of last summer and tossing waves off the Kerry coast.

Peader didn't really notice how pale and beautiful the beach was. He was observing the road, his head full of Michael Gillespie's mythology. 'Roger Casement, a homosexual, arrived on Banna Strand, 1916, was arrested and hanged.' Items of Michael's history lessons returned.

When Peader was twelve, he was adopted by Michael, brought to his house near the pier and was given a room, alien to him, told by Michael to be calm and often, a little harrassed, make his way back to his father's caravan where his father beat his brother Johnny.

The first time Michael referred to Roger Casement as being a homosexual Peader didn't know what the word meant. He must have been twelve or thirteen when Michael spoke about Casement and it was probably spring as spring was a penetrating season in the west of Ireland, lobster pots reeking of tensed trapped lobster.

When he was seventeen and running away, Peader still knew little about the word, more about a love affair with Michael.

A donkey stood out before them. 'I'll tell him to go away,' Sandra said.

She got out, hugging the donkey's brown skin, kissing his nose, and Peader watched, silenced.

Why was he thinking of Michael now? Why the silence between him and Sandra?

Perhaps because he felt he'd soon see Michael again.

They were going to a festival in Kerry; Peader had given up his job in Belfast and Sandra and he had bought antiques cheap and with a van full of them were going to sell them at the festival which included plays, dancing, lectures, music, drinking and most of all the picking of a festival queen.

Kerry had many festivals, at all times of the year and since Peader's family originally came from Kerry he'd make his way back there at odd times, like the time in London he threw up his job on a site and went to Dingle for the summer, sleeping in a half-built house, a house abandoned by a Dublin politician who had thoughts of living there when it was fashionable and when it ceased being fashionable with his mates, he abandoned the place in time for summer and Peader's stay there.

'We'll have a good time,' Sandra thought. 'We'll have a good time.' She was smoking a cigarette she'd picked up in a café in Limerick, her head slouched so that her hair fell across her face.

'How long is it?'

'Ten miles.'

Her mouth pouted. Her resistance was low; there was a

strangeness about Peader. This she knew. Her silence deepened. Cigarette-smoking was a token activity.

Maybe it was because of his return to roots Peader was silent. Perhaps he felt sad on coming back to Kerry and the towns of big houses and the verandas of hotels which held rare flowers because it was warm nearly all the year round in Kerry, a gulf stream climate.

'There's a rhododendron,' she shouted.

The first she'd seen that year but Peader wasn't interested and she said to herself 'maybe there's things I don't know'.

She wasn't really a tinker; she'd grown up in Ballyfermot in Dublin. Her father sold junk, broken furniture, broken chairs, broken clocks and her cousin played a tin-whistle and was married to a Mayo tinker, playing in Germany for a living.

He was famous now, having gone to Berlin, barely knowing how to sing but by some fluke ending up in a night-spot in a West Berlin bar. Now he had two records and his wife often sang with him, a wild woman with black hair who gave Sandra's family an association with tinker stock.

Sandra had met Peader at a Sinn Féin hop. Neither Sandra nor Peader had any interests in politics but both had cousins and uncles who supported Sinn Féin and God knows what else, maybe guns and bombing and the blowing up in the North.

Sandra had a Belfast side to her family, her mother's side, and though her mother was silent about Belfast grief, Sandra knew of cousins in the North who wore black berets and dark glasses and accompanied funeral victims, often men who'd died in action. Sandra's main association with the North was tomato ketchup spilling the day she heard her cousin John was dead, a little boy run down by an ambulance which had been screaming away from the debris of a bombing.

She'd seen Peader at the Sinn Féin hop, a boy sitting down, eyes on the ground. A woman with dyed hair sang 'I left my heart in San Francisco' and a girl with biting Derry accent sang 'Roddy McCordy', a Fenian ballad.

Peader asked her to dance – they'd hardly spoken, his hands left an imprint on her back and on ladies' choice she asked him up; his fingers tightened a little awkwardly about her. The girl from Derry sang 'Four Green Fields' as the lights dimmed; a song about Mother Ireland's grief at the loss of her fourth field, Ulster.

People clapped and there was a collection for internees in Long Kesh but Sandra and Peader slipped away; he slept in her house, on the sofa in the sitting room.

He told her he was just back from England, his first time in four years. He seemed upset, gnome-like as he was drinking coffee in her home.

She sensed a sorrow but sorrow was never mentioned between them, not even when they were going to films at the Adelphi or when they eventually married, the wedding taking place at the church in Stephen's Green, her family outside, black-haired; his, the remnants from Connemara and Kerry, his brother dressed like Elvis Presley and his cousins and second cousins in a mad array of suits, hair wild on women in prim suits bought at Listowel or Galway for the occasion.

Come winter they went to Belfast, Sandra's Uncle Martin providing Peader with work. Springfield Road where they lived ran through a Catholic area, then a Protestant area, again a Catholic area.

Its colour was dark and bloody. Like its history. Catholic boys walked by in blue. Protestant boys walked by in blue. One wouldn't know the difference. Yet they killed one another, violence ran up and down the road and on in the hills at the top of the road a boy was found crucified one day, a child of ten gagged to a cross by other children of ten, his hands twisted with rope and he half-dead and sobbing.

'We'll leave Belfast,' Sandra said one day, crying over the newspaper. A little girl had been killed down the road by a bomb planted in a transistor set.

'Where do we go?' Peader brooded on the question.

He came up with an answer, drove back in their van one

day loaded with antiques from a bombed out shop. Together they procured more; 'my father used to buy and sell things at the Ballinasloe fair,' Peader said, 'I can take a hint.'

His father and his father's father sold things like grandfather clocks in North Kerry. His father moved to Connemara on marrying Brigid Ward, his mother, and she dying on a wild Connemara night, after he beating her, left her two children, John, Peader. Peader was the one taken by the poet; Peader now with what Sandra observed as ancestral intelligence returned to the feel of country things – clocks, paintings of women in white writhing as though in pain – to the purchasing and reselling of these items.

A man waved. Women wandered through the streets, country women, all loaded with bags and with the air of those who'd come from fresh land and flowered gardens. They'd arrived.

'Let's park the van,' said Peader. Sandra had long since forgotten her troubles but on seeing a young man, a Romany maybe, with black falling hair, a cravat of red and white and an earring pierced in his right ear, gold, she wondered at their purpose in coming here and felt what she could only decide was fright.

Through the day women with plants walked past their stall, geraniums dancing in pots and women laughing. Business went well.

Craftily Peader sold his wares, producing more, the mementoes of County Antrim unionists disappearing here in the Kerry market town.

Relatives of Peader appeared from nowhere, his father's people. Mickey-Joe, Joseph-James, Eoghan-Liam. Men from Kenmare and Killarney.

They'd been to Kerry for their honeymoon, Sandra and Peader, but for the most part Kerry was unknown to Sandra apart from Peader's accounts of childhood visits here from Connemara, to Dingle and Kenmare, to the wild desolate Ballinskelligs peninsula full of ghost villages, graves, to Dún Caoin and the impending view of the Blaskets and Skellig

Mhicel and the Sleeping Monk, an island which looked like a monk in repose.

'Sandra, my wife.' People shook her hand; grievously some did it, men were hurt by lack of sex. He took her hand. They were in a crowded pub and Peader stroked first Sandra's thumb, then took her whole hand and rubbed it.

'You've had too much,' said Sandra, but already he was slipping away. She was far from him.

In his mind, Peader saw Michael Gillespie making his way through the crowd that day. Michael hadn't seen him but Peader remained strangely frightened, fearful of an encounter.

All the poets and playwrights of Ireland seemed to be here for it was a festival of writers too, writers reading from their work, writers lecturing.

In the pub now Michael entered. He stood, shocked. His black hair smitten on his forehead. There was no sense of effeteness about him as there used to be. He was all there, brooding, brilliant in middle-age, ageless almost.

'Hello.'

Peader shook his head – tremulously. So tremulously that he thought of shaking rose bushes in Michael's garden in Connemara when Peader was fourteen or fifteen, frightened by rain, by shaking things.

'Michael, this is my wife, Sandra.'

Michael looked towards her and smiled. He had on a many-coloured T-shirt. 'Your wife.'

Five years since they'd met; it all cascaded now. Peader asked Michael if he wanted a drink but Michael insisted on buying drinks for both of them, Guinness heavily topped with cream.

'To your beautiful wife,' Michael toasted Sandra.

He was here to read his poems he explained, he had a new book out.

'Did you win any more prizes?' Peader asked.

'Not recently,' Michael replied. But he'd opened a crafts shop in Connemara and anyway he lectured widely now, streaming off to universities in Chicago or in Texas. He had a world-wide following.

'Good to be famous,' Peader said.

'Alone?' Michael questioned.

Sandra was now talking to a boy with a Dublin accent; he had on a cravat and they chatted gaily, obviously having found some acquaintance in common.

'Your wife is lovely.' Remarks loaded, laden with other comment.

Eventually Michael said – sportingly almost.

'How was it?'

'What?'

'London.'

'All right.'

'Big?'

'At my age, yes.'

'You managed.'

'I was careful.'

Michael looked at him. 'You look OK.'

Peader remembered the times he was thirteen, Michael minding him, giving him honey in the mornings, eggs fresh, little banquets of eggs with yellow flowing tops.

He remembered the time he was fourteen, by which time Michael had seduced him. He remembered the white pillow and in summer the grey morning that would merge into the big room and afterwards the excitement of sailing a boat or running on the sand.

'Your daddy wouldn't like it!' Michael said one day and Peader thought back to winter and the roadside caravan and his hairy father frying mutton chops that smelt like rabbits dead and rotting.

'You're more handsome than ever.'

'Am I?'

'Tough!'

'Married.'

'Your wife is lovely.'

'You said.'

'I can't say it too much. She's got a gorgeous smile.'

'What have you been doing?'

'Working, writing, lecturing. For two years I lived with an American student from Carolina, a Spanish-American girl.'

'Black-haired?'

'Yes.'

'I thought you preferred them blonde.'

'Who?'

'People.'

'Peader, you've become harsh.'

Harsh. The winters were often harsh in Connemara; when Peader was fifteen it snowed and he and Michael freed a fox from a trap near a farm-yard. Peader's hair was quite blond then and rode his head like a heavy shield against the elements.

'This won't last forever,' Michael said one day, weeping.

Peader had emptied a bowl of chestnuts into the gutter at Hallowe'en. In a temper, often Peader could be brazen and perhaps it was his brazenness which drove him to run away.

It was after he'd had an affair with a girl from Clifden, cut through her thighs in a barn near the sea; in a corduroy suit with his trousers down found woman nearer to satisfaction than man.

He ran away to London, a city of many women and found no one there interested in him.

No one beyond the odd foreman on a building site and a man from Kerry who gave him rudimentary training in carpentry and in skills of tradesmanship.

'Are you going to see the festival queen crowned?' Michael asked.

'Yes,' Peader nudged Sandra. 'Will we go and see the festival queen crowned?'

Sandra turned to him. 'Yes. Here's John from Dublin.'

The Dublin boy shook hands with them. They made a party, trailing off.

'Is that the man that brought you up?' Sandra nudged Peader.

'Yes.' His reply was drowned by the crowd, noise, mingling, bunting shaking in the bustling avenues, old women crying raucously and the young holding one another.

They made their way to a square where the queen was just being crowned, a woman who looked like Marilyn Monroe, her smile big and awkward. Cheers rose about them and fights broke out.

Peader felt himself stirring with an old passion; how many times in bed with Sandra had he longed again to be fondled by male hands, and the points of adolescence, his knees, his genitals, to be fondled in the old way.

Instead of having a mother, he'd had Michael. Instead of adolescent tears and rashness, there'd been an even flow, card games, winkle-picking, mountain climbs, a spiral of strange fulfilment.

As the crowd jostled Peader felt Michael's nervous hand on his shoulder. 'Is your wife having a child?'

'Not yet.'

'Someday?'

'Seed is a strange thing,' Michael said; his words nearly drowned. 'The seed that seems lost but is devoured by an artist's vision, an artist's uncertainty, the uncertainty of reaching to people, the feeling of trying and failing and trying again and loving someone – anyone.'

'Me?'

'Yes – you were the one.'

A balloon went into the air. It slipped into the air, red, against a rather retiring-looking moon. The fireworks went off, splattered against the sky.

'Like a monstrance at mass,' Peader thought, remembering childhood and the times his father would take him to mass in Clifden, the priest turning with a golden, sun-like object to his congregation and the people bowing like slaves.

Peader virtually hadn't been to mass since he was seven – except the odd ceremony – like his wedding.

'Let's go somewhere,' Michael said.

'Peader, I've missed you, I've missed your arms and your

65

body. I've waited for you. You can see poems I've written about you and read at Oxford and Cambridge.'

'Sandra,' Peader was going to call out to her but she was lost among the crowd with the boy from Dublin.

At three o'clock that morning Sandra made her way back to the tent she and Peader had erected that day. How would she tell Peader? It had been so strange meeting John, a boy from Ballyfermot she'd dated at fifteen. He'd turned into a buxom motorbike hippie; his pink shirt had drooped open that evening revealing a strongly tanned chest.

'We're all gipsies,' John had said, 'we people from Ballyfermot.'

Ballyfermot, a working-class suburb of Dublin.

She'd lost Peader and the man he was talking to in a crowd, rather strange enigmatic Englishman, and found herself adrift with John.

They'd found their way to a pub which was situated beside a tin caravan where fish and chips were being served, and there in the pub had hot whiskeys, and recalled going to James Bond films in the Savoy together before John's motorbike vocation and Sandra's wedding. John had found money in his travels; he'd lived with an old rich Italian lady near Trieste.

'Festivals bring strange people together,' Sandra had said, getting drunker and drunker, leaning on John's leather jacket.

The tent was forgotten and Peader and the rather strange Englishman who had his arms about Peader, the man Peader had often referred to in rather sharp clipped sentences. She'd ended up lying on John's stomach.

'Let's go to the mountains,' John had said.

'No, to the sea.' Her order was relieved by her mounting the bike and making to the sea. Waves surged in and she ran beside them and John recounted more and more of his experiences in Europe, a night in Nice with a millionaire's daughter, striding by the Mediterranean on the sea-walk below the city with a bottle of champagne.

'Let's make love,' John hugged her.

She relapsed into his arms and lay with him on the sand but didn't stir to embrace him further, knowing that her faithfulness wasn't to John and the affairs of adolescence but to Peader and his toughness.

Making her way back to the tent, she thought of Peader and the difference between her and him, a difference she hadn't realized until that night, meeting John again; she'd realized and wondered at the fields of her childhood, fields on the outskirts of Dublin where tinker caravans were often encamped and which snow brushed in winter, fields grabbed by Dublin's ever-expanding suburbs. Peader had come from a different world, a world of nature continued, ever-present, ever-flowing.

He came from the sea and the west, a world of fury.

There'd been different laws there, different accidents, a savagery of robins dying in winter snow and scarecrows looking like the faces of the people, faces starved for want of love.

Coming towards the tent she heard voices within, male voices. A thought struck her that Peader was inside with the Englishman whom he'd been talking to earlier in the evening. It had been a strange, packed way they'd been talking; Peader's clipped sentences returned to Sandra. 'The day Michael and I walked to the sea', 'the day Michael and I went sailing', 'the day Michael and I collected blackberries'.

Sandra stopped and listened outside the tent. There was a low moan of pain and Sandra began shaking.

It wasn't cold but she was sure now of Peader's past; she knew him to be a traitor. He came from a world of lies.

'Peader,' she pulled back the drape of the tent and inside she saw Peader, arm in arm with a young boy she'd never seen before.

She began running but there was a sudden clench, Peader stopped her.

He was naked and wet. He took her forehead and he took her face.

He kissed her throat and her neck and his tongue dabbed in her mouth. And she fell before him into the cold, dirt-laden path.

His big and eager face loomed before her. 'It's all right, Sandra,' he said.

'I had to do it and I couldn't hide it from you. There's things to be done and said in life; you must go back, sometimes.'

She'd never know how Michael Gillespie had tried to seduce Peader that night, she'd never know how Peader had repulsed him and walked away, drunk through the crowd.

She'd never know how Peader had picked up a young boy from Cahirciveen who'd been drunkenly urinating and made love to him in the tent, kissed his white naked pimples as Michael Gillespie had kissed his years before.

She'd never know but when she woke in the morning between Peader and a young boy she knew more about life's passion than she'd ever known before. She rose and put on a long skirt and looked at the morning, fresh, blue-laden, as she'd never seen it before.

Portrait of a Dancer

His mother sat over the fire warming her palms. She stared, merely stared. Colours furiously froze and spat.

She sat in blue. Her hair now was tinged with grey but still held a marmalade colour; right now it was brightened and delighted with flame. She sat pondering her own beauty. He stood by the door, lingering, waiting for her to notice him but she didn't, she continued to stare, continued to ponder, continued to absorb.

'Mother.' She turned. 'Damian.' She was not surprised to see him. 'How are you?' 'Well.' He lay down his books. 'Tired?' 'No.' She moved towards the table. 'I have duckling. I hope you don't mind it being a bit burnt.'

He sat down, ate.

'Well, how's it going?'

'Well.'

Two months at art school he was already frittering his time. Bored, he was drawing nudes without much conviction.

His career was chequered to say the least. His mother's need to move had caused his childhood to be a stream of cities, nucleus of colours, white of desert sands, neon of downtown New York. His mother had been an original New Yorker, a model in the 1940s until she met an Irish poet who fathered him. The poet had died early, of drink. His marriage had been unperturbed by the affair. A woman had mourned him, his wife. Damian's mother had nourished her own grief quietly, first in New York, then in a variety of places, passing among the rich and the famous.

He'd been sent to school first in Marrakesh, then in Scotland in a free school.

Out of school six months he'd begun at art school, his mother settled now, less than serene, in a London apartment. She hung a picture of herself over the fireplace, one in which the world could see her as pretty. It was a reproduction of a painting by an eminent modern artist housed in a New York art gallery. In the painting her neck swung towards her nape like a swan's neck. Her eyes rang with laughter. Her face was thin and pinched and her lips smote the vision like a paper rose.

'Damian, did you have a good day?'

'Yes.' Then he said, 'No. No I didn't.'

He went to bed early reading Chekhov, sleeping with it on his chest.

The first time he met her was in November. She was late coming to the school, an Irish art teacher. She was about thirty-two, had black hair, carved like a Cretan. 'She was pretty,' Damian thought to himself, New York expressions still in his head, American gentleness.

She taught him to paint. She hovered across his figure, staring downwards. He enjoyed her closeness and often wondered at her face, being Irish it should have spoken of violence.

Instead it was calm – like the Book of Kells which Damian had once seen in Dublin, lying open in Trinity College.

She was from Connemara. The name sung in Damian's ears. His father had lived there, a father he'd never met, just heard about.

'Hi.' He spoke to her one day in the canteen. She approached, looking through him almost.

They spoke. They mentioned backgrounds. They parted.

That night Damian realized he was in love.

His mother sat by the fire as though in prayer.

She sat staring into the flame.

'How are you?'

'Well.'

He went to his room and packed his clothes. He was moving out.

His mother sat as usual by the fire when he returned from school on the following days.

He told her he was going and she hardly seemed perturbed.

'Where are you going?'

'To squat in West Harrow.'

His mother shrugged. 'Don't get cold whatever you do.' The squat consisted of high Edwardian buildings, fronted by rubbish dumps.

Damian got a room in one of them with the assistance of a friend. First he tacked a picture of Pablo Casals on the wall.

Then he arranged a matted quilt on the bed. The quilt was multi-coloured. He would sleep beneath colours.

There was a fireplace in the room and he lit warm fires in the afternoons, sitting beside them with a warm rugged polo-neck on.

He usually tracked down the Irish teacher on her way to the bus, dwelling a few minutes in conversation with her as leaves merely rested on dusty earth.

He was going to ask her out. He planned it for weeks.

The squat in which he lived housed runaway girls who wore long black coats and big Edwardian hats. Their maroon and pink colours dashed into afternoons of black sidling rain. 'I want to make love,' Damian told himself, 'I want to make love to this woman.'

He invited her to tea one day.

She was at first surprised by the invitation. Then she accepted.

'I'd love to,' she said.

He bought a cake iced in a Jewish bakery and they ate sweet things.

She left early. He watched her go and knew how deep was his attraction for her. An attraction to calm, simplicity, the hush her voice was.

His mother had joined a mystical group and was reading

71

the words of Greek and Russian mysticists. Years previously she had known a man in California who had known the mentor of her group, Gurdjieff, and this single fragment had inspired enough confidence to move, search. She was going out again and very, very slowly talking about her travels and her affairs and her intimacies with artists, widely known and little heard of.

The teacher came to Damian one day, uninvited. She brought with her tomatoes.

She took off her gloves and her coat.

'I hope you don't mind me calling,' she said.

He smiled. 'I suppose I was feeling lonely today,' she said.

'Lonely?' He laughed. 'Do you miss Ireland?'

'I was hurt by Ireland,' she said. He didn't ask her anymore but made tea and smiled at her and poised Tchaikovsky on the record player he'd recently bought. 'These days my mother talks of Central Park,' Damian said. 'It's like as though it's a womb.'

Madeleine – the teacher – looked at his ring. 'It's lovely,' she said. 'Silver?'

'Yes.' She stared at him. 'It's good to know someone I can come to see.' He took her hand.

He kissed it. She withdrew, shivered almost. He moved towards her. In moments they were lovers.

They made love from love. This was an experience never to be repeated. It was her world and his that merged, the colours, sombre, green, of Ireland, the mad dash of kaleidoscopic colours which had been Damian's travels.

They looked at one another afterwards, recognizing friendship, friendship never to be repeated.

She rose, put on her clothes, walked away. He stood with her outside a seven-day adventist church, attending a bus. Her brow was furrowed. He was willing to wait for a long time, he was willing to wait until an eternity. He wanted to tell her that together they'd discovered what his mother had never found in her travels – the experience of creativity. But before he could open his mouth a bus came and she was

72

taken from him, chocolate papers brushed the pavement already wet with afternoon rain.

His mother was reading Isaiah when he called. 'And the leopard shall lie down with the kid,' she said snapping the book closed, almost accusing Damian. Damian quietly made tea while she talked about his father, the poet, times with him in retreat in the west of Ireland. 'A highly illicit affair,' she declared almost shouting.

Damian ate sweet cakes which his mother fetched from a confectionery shop in Soho. Damian stared at the flames, penetratingly. He knew that moment that he, a person without a country, his mother, also a person without a country, were now crossing paths, realizing that one moment of love could exonerate one of a life of loneliness.

He saw her often. She came to his house and they slept in the big bed and they spoke about countries by firelight.

She whispered. 'Someone told me I was frigid in Ireland. They said I was frigid to hurt me. You have repaired me.' Damian was drinking cocoa. 'They told me I was frigid because I was rather spiritual, because I kept to myself and observed certain laws, laws of solitude, laws I hoped of love. The Irish are a people at war with themselves. England has given me an order.'

He turned to her, momentarily observed pain, pursed his lips and looked again at the stars, little silver stars sparkling and spitting in the flame.

At Christmas she returned to Ireland. He walked her to Euston and observed her board a train and felt very much the young lover with his genitals ringing as wheels clattered. He walked away, hoping the Guinness pubs would not defile her and when she returned she spoke of change, the rosettes of white houses in Connemara, new buildings, new blood.

She spoke of having seen a punk-rock band play in a hall which lay among fields where stones were gilded with moon and how she saw toothless couples dance to the mad murderous music. They made love, out of a hush, out of a

73

calm left by conversation. They renewed physical contact and then Madeleine wept and she wished she could return to Ireland but defiled by it she was an exile at heart, an exile in abeyance to wounds.

Wood crackled in January as they sat on Saturday afternoons drinking coffee, talking, the photograph of Pablo Casals curling up in agony.

'I knew a girl at school,' Damian said, 'who had long hair and played a guitar and would run across fields like a fairy. Sometimes we'd just sit on the grass not saying anything, just holding hands.'

'School is the most creative experience of one's life,' Madeleine said. 'God speaks to us at secondary school, light through the doorway, a plant on the window, a picture of Joan Baez playing guitar in Birmingham, Alabama.'

'God?'

'Yes. Is that what's troubling all of us? Your mother, me, you; it is a terrible thing to believe, worse to doubt.'

'Aren't we all being driven by a force asking us for a simple gesture, a simple pain that is close to a real experience, an experience of life.'

His mother was happier now, thrilled almost.

Men and women were drifting into her apartment, supping coffee, discussing art, literature, religion. She was relinquishing her solitude and inviting the strands of her life, mislaid, to meet again. Her son came among these people, black knotted hair, a white shirt on him, his lips succulent. He was an added treat, youth, beauty remembered by all of them in circles in California where men spoke of Buddha or Indian philosophers emerging from the rain forests to speak of God to post-war dilettantes.

In February Damian told his mother he was having an affair. His mother took it philosophically until Damian mentioned his lover was Irish. Then his mother whispered, 'They're a cruel race, a cruel race.'

She was ill for a few days and when she returned to school Damian asked her if she'd accompany him to Greece.

'Greece!'

Early Easter holidays were approaching.

'We could get a bus.'

She'd been ill, she said over coffee, she'd stayed in bed.

'Why didn't you come to see me?'

Damian paused. He realized it had not occurred to him. He'd been in Madeleine's bedsitter but once. It was her custom to come to him. He'd never expected otherwise.

'I'm sorry.'

'You're used to being looked after,' Madeleine said. 'Yes, I'll go with you.'

He painted through March and was influenced much by Chagall whom his mother met in Vence once when he shook her hand with his pale, pale Russian hand.

He brought Madeleine to little cinemas and he cycled to school on an old bicycle picked up in Portobello Road.

On a grey day in March they caught a bus from Argylle Road to Athens, crossing Europe through snow and rain and reaching an island by boat where blossoms were shaping like curls on a baby's head.

They lived in a whitewashed cottage for three weeks, the sea daily becoming bluer and Madeleine's hair falling on her shoulders now and her face a sort of cow-like serenity.

'You're too young for me, you know,' she said over retsina one evening. Damian looked at her. He knew she was going to say that and that she'd just been holding back, waiting for this moment, watching Greeks, watching donkeys, watching priests with beards blowing in March breezes.

Madeleine's head dipped. She took hold of her wine glass like a pistol.

'I have been reading Chekhov,' she said. 'I found this quotation.' She read, almost in a murmur. ' "I don't believe in our intelligentsia. I believe in individual people scattered here and there all over Russia – they have strength though they are few." '

'Meaning?'

'That lives cross briefly, that we are in danger of losing

ourselves unless we make supreme acts, reach out, know where to stop.'

'Like my mother,' Damian said.

'Like your mother, coming, going between people. The trouble is she never knew where to stop. But she has searched.'

Madeleine quietened. 'She has searched.'

They walked by the strand where the light on the sea reminded Madeleine of Connemara and where they spoke of the Atlantic where Madeleine came from, and where Damian's mother holidayed with Damian's secret father.

'The sea wills a strange power on us,' Madeleine said, 'a power of believing.'

They held hands and strode along until Damian quietly announced it was Easter Sunday and that it was believed Christ had risen on this day.

Back in London they saw one another less. In May Madeleine lived with him for a week and they slept in the big bed under the multi-coloured quilt, and made love, his body seeking hers as though she was an immense bear, shielding him.

Then one morning she left – discreetly – before he woke and he saw her only at school after that. She didn't go home with him. She acted older than him, determined on the course of her life, refusing solicitude.

He was shattered. He pursued her with his eyes. She never acknowledged him. She studied the work of her students and left his looks unrequited, and when he followed her she said, 'Damian, it's unwise to go ahead with certain things. Forget it. Forget it.'

'What are you doing for the summer?' he asked.

'Going back to Ireland. I think I can come to terms with it now. I think I can get to know it.'

'Might you stay there?'

'Perhaps. England is not my country. They tell us Irish we're bombers whereas it's a few British subjects from the North who are planting bombs. I think I'll go home, teach in a small school, marry a farmer.'

'Madeleine, please come home with me,' he begged her.

'Damian,' she turned. 'Find yourself some nice nineteen-year-old.'

He could have killed himself. Instead he went to his mother. She was drinking brandy and saying sweetly to herself. 'Life is beautiful. Life is a collection of moods, moods, fine, peaceable, attractive. Life is a coloured shadow. Life is a coloured shadow.'

Damian realized she was quoting the Irish poet who'd been her lover. He went to his room and asked of it what he'd done wrong, realized that this impermanence was just living and decided to go south again for the summer.

He didn't go south. Instead he went to Ireland where he hitched about, taking in Cork and Limerick, finding no trace of her but discovering mountains wild and blue, and sheep, rinsed yellow ochre and white. He sat in cafés thinking of her as American tourists clambered after tweed and would have asked the skies to show her to him had he not realized that was rather over-romantic and that anyway she was in another part of Ireland, one as yet unknown to him. He didn't go to Connemara because heavy squally rain began and wouldn't stop and he found himself one August morning in London, drinking steaming coffee.

In September back at school he discovered she had not stayed in Ireland, that she was teaching at another school and when he heard she was playing in an amateur production of Yeats's *Herne's Egg* at the school he went to see her in it. He caught a bus from the squat, through streets swishing with rain where girls in long coats and Edwardian hats ran.

He sat in the auditorium as she danced the part of Attracta, priestess of love, sombrely, fatalistically.

'She was Irish,' he told himself, 'she had been driven out again by a word, a look, a gesture back to London.'

Afterwards he waited in the caféteria for her, in his white-blue embroidered shirt, whispering under his breath, 'I love you. I love you. I love you,' and when she didn't come he went home, took up a knife to cut his wrists and suddenly, just suddenly found himself pardoned by the glowing of the fire, which caught the knife, telling him sonorously of travels, travels through lives, faces, bodies, travels which wrought images of Irish women with black Cretan hair and faces that always looked as though about to give way or of women of middle age sitting by the fire, telling themselves over and over again that life was beautiful as flame glinted and eyes spat and hair that was grey turned gold.

The Birth of Laughter

Walking through the garden she carefully chided the trees, pulling bushes from her way, distracting leaves from her hair. That she was back here hardly made sense to her. That she was unafraid was not safe to contemplate. Being here was easy. She looked about. Light stole through her hair. She was twenty-two. An observer would have considered her to be very beautiful, hair twisted and knotted in gold pigtails.

A butterfly rose. She stared, haunted by the pallor of its wings. She laughed. The child inside her would be a girl, a brown girl like the black babies in Roman Catholic national schools, nodding on boxes which were filled with money for the foreign missions. The butterfly waved, danced, coaxed. She ran. Her hand reached towards it. Light caught her topaz ring. The colours in it sparkled, green, orange, brown. Catherine laughed. She laughed until the entire garden heard her laughter. Her body froze. Was she really laughing? Was this voice really hers? She waited. Nothing happened. No one took her. A blind aftermath of laughter rang through her. She laughed again, raced again until the entire garden welled with imaginary butterflies and her hair spun imaginary roses.

She stopped. She walked. She felt trees again, bushes again, a Lazarus reborn to sensation. She walked slowly as though in a trance. It was like slow motion in a childhood film. Catherine Findlater you are reborn to the exquisite touch of things she told herself. Catherine Findlater you are saved.

The grass by the stream was already gold. Some straws

held themselves high like August wheat. She knelt by the water. Her face glowed. She smiled. She smudged her features with her fingers. She smiled again. Laughter was imminent. This time she did not laugh. She screamed. A figure rose behind her. She looked up quickly. It was Adoe. He embraced her. His skin was stretched and light brown over brittle bones. His arm held her to him. His shirt was white. They strolled through the garden. In lighter moments of remembrance she could recall Aunt Madeleine reciting lines of balmy love poetry by her friend William Butler Yeats or the Song of Solomon, or having recourse to Byron. She strolled now with her Indian lover and husband. Laburnum was bursting, lilac already sheathing bushes with white.

'You're all right. You're fine,' he said.

Sometimes she'd stare at him and ask him why he'd brought her here. 'You must come back. For your own good.' She was frightened and crying. She'd been left the house by her Aunt Madeleine. True she'd grown fond of the lilac there. True she'd placed a big rubber doll among the snowdrops there, left it languishing, sticking pins into it, hoping to draw blood to colour the snowdrops red. In other words she'd been a child here. But the resting place of Aunt Madeleine's shorn-out heart was too close for comfort, grey Wexford stone.

In a Dublin flat she'd said 'No. I can't go back. I can't.' One night when Adoe was out performing in a play – *Ghosts* by Ibsen – she'd risen screaming. The whole ritual had risen in her. She'd begun sweating. She'd been a month pregnant. She'd gone to the window. It had been in Fitzwilliam Square. She'd pushed up the frame. Sweat was emerging like a shadow from her skin. She'd wished herself dead upon the pavement below. She'd made to throw herself. He'd caught her. He'd forced her on the bed. He'd made love to her. Her mind had given way. She'd dreamt of mice, many mice in the castle long ago. Mice were crawling at her feet. Mice were running beneath and betwixt her. She'd woken as though to scream. He'd been beside her. She'd smitten his nipple with her right forefinger. It had been a butterfly. It had come alive to her. She'd kissed it. She'd slept upon his stomach.

A real butterfly waved by now. 'Look,' she cried delightedly. 'Isn't it pretty.' 'She,' Adoe corrected her. 'It's a she. A she butterfly.' 'How do you know?' 'Isn't it obvious?'

Whereas the previous butterfly had been merely white this one was many coloured. 'Lovely,' Catherine cried. 'Lovely. Lovely. Lovely.' She turned to Adoe. His lips burgeoned with a red like summer raspberries. She kissed him. He held her. Her laughter became tears now; tears shook from her. Again the fear rose in her. She stared into the density of Adoe's chocolate brown eyes. 'Do not forsake me.' 'No,' his voice was a whisper. The french windows behind her held a shadow of lace. Catherine began sobbing and as she did the french windows splintered with red, red from a drawing-room geranium. 'Adoe,' she clutched him. The child started coming. She held him. She collapsed.

Avenues of cypresses in the summer sun; these were her first memories. These cypresses darkened; they held back – like a deluge. Her mother would take her hand, dolled up in grey skirt and white blouse and persuade her through these shadows. Catherine would look – scared. Her mother had been a parson's daughter from Offaly, singularly quiet and inoffensive. She'd married George Findlater after meeting him at a midsummer's party in Tipperary, south of Offaly, north of Wexford. The party had occurred beside a lake. The hills had been lit by fires, burning for St John's Eve, bronzed young men, disgorging themselves of shirts, jumping over the flames, and shadows of flame and evening fire imminent on the lake. The man she'd met had been attractive, rather like one would imagine Emily Brontë's father to have been attractive. He'd been distant and contemplative of the sunset; they'd courted. He'd driven from Wexford in a Ford coupé which resembled a ricocheted funeral car. They'd married when apples had been burnished in the County Wexford glades of George's home. They'd honeymooned in Galway; on a lake beside a convent school where nuns wandered about reading breviaries, draped like blue whales. They'd made love. They'd conceived Catherine there. They'd returned to Wexford.

'There has been much suffering in the Findlater family,' her mother had always said to Catherine. If one looked one could see the offset of such suffering on her mother's face. She'd arrived in Wexford to live in a lowly decaying castle. Portraits had exploded about her like decaying cartoons. Suits of armour had astonished her with their glamour of light. More than anything she'd been awed by the garden, by the richness of shade there, by the effervescence of grass. She'd stare as Madeleine held her parties.

To these parties would be drawn the élite of Ireland and Britain, young men with faint gladness, neckties and cravats bursting. These young men came from the hills, from the Midlands, from castles and fortresses, the last of the Anglo-Irish peers. They'd come with wolfhounds, with gangling strides, with fat and expensive cigars whose odours suggested Berlin and Paris. Madeleine would entertain them with the full force of the servant population of the house. She'd lay tables with cakes and strawberries and cream, escalating cakes, bilberry wines; lavender and roses decorating the sheer white and the sheer length of the table. One could hear her voice cackle. 'The horn of plenty,' she'd cry and Catherine's mother daily becoming more and more aware of local resentment, realized that Findlaters' access to wealth was based on famine, on centuries-old greed. Once a Findlater had wandered to Ireland in dainty pantaloons with Edmund Spenser, recognized this valley with its rolling glades and gossamer-like hawthorn as being a place of serenity, set up home here, ransacked the district, drew much wealth to the house. The Findlaters had lost their title through a row with Queen Victoria and some of them had taken to the church, a black whispering Protestantism. During the famine the family was beset by wraith-like peasants haranguing the door like famished wolfhounds. They received potatoes, soup. Their eyes haunted the occupants of the house like the dots on a peacock's feather. 'Remember 1798,' the eyes seemed to say. 'Remember the young men who rode into your garden and died among the apple-blossoms, wounded in Wexford by the Redcoats.' Maids would firmly replace the leaden locks, shutting out the offending evenings of famine Ireland.

'The horn of plenty!' Madeleine's voice reverberated through the garden even after she'd taken up her bags and flown to Paris in an aeroplane from Shannon airport. 'The horn of plenty!' Catherine's mother had been haunted by Madeleine's silken clothes as she'd wandered about the castle. In the same year her husband had died of a heart attack, she herself had begun to grow weaker and George's two sisters, living in two separate houses in the village had taken to flights of madness, wandering in the night, both in nightgowns, speaking of ghosts, of wolfhounds, of legendary Irish heroes. Both had been diverted to a mental hospital in Enniscorthy where they ate fresh tomatoes and stared, blissfully, and hauntedly, at the river below. George's third sister, Madeleine, likewise owning a small house in the village, had disappeared to Paris, so as Catherine grew up, holding her mother's hand as she strolled down avenues of cypress trees, all she'd known of Aunt Madeleine was an awesome photograph in the livingroom, Madeleine's hair long and black and flowing and her lips, smiling even in middle-age, flushed and shot through as though by blood.

These were her earliest memories, sitting in the living-room in winter or summer, her mother reading her huge handsome volumes of Hans Christian Andersen or the Grimm brothers. If it were summer the windows would be open and bees singing across the patterns of the carpet. If it were winter huge fires would be rumbling and Catherine's mother would occasionally lean towards the blaze and pick chestnuts from the turf. Then her mother died. Catherine had been five. She died almost as gently and as devotedly as ogres came and went in fairy stories or as young women with long golden hair had been carried off to round towers where they waited for handsome princes to free them.

The cause of death – later established – was a lung complaint. Catherine watched her burial. It had been winter. She clutched a doll and shed some tears and watched water springing like seeds from branches. It had been raining. Servants were there in force. Wexford spread. 'If one looked far enough,' Catherine had thought, 'one could see strawberries.'

As a rule strawberries did not arrive in Wexford until June. That year had been no exception. Catherine had waited for strawberries, their seedling red, and knew also that her Aunt Madeleine, previously unidentified, was arriving to look after her. All she'd known of Aunt Madeleine was her books, her photograph. It was known Aunt Madeleine was the author of books. They lingered in the house – like ghosts.

She arrived one afternoon, drawing up in a hearse-like taxi. Her face had seemed blotched and bewildered. Catherine had stared, teddy bear loose in her fingers. Madeleine had beheld her. Her eyes had a lucidity and yet a horror which burnt into memory.

Madeleine Findlater, authoress, author of historical romances, a study of the tarot and a biography of an obscure Rumanian poet who died in 1937.

Catherine's eyes opened – she was in a hospital. Nurses studied her. There was one who held a glass of water. She recognized Adoe behind a black doctor. She reached for him. She collapsed.

Five years old she'd been then and innocent of her aunt's past. The castle was sold to an American millionaire who brought a blue-haired mistress to convalesce there from an attack of polio and who then abandoned it, allowing snowdrops in spring to overshadow its lawns, a lonely cold twirling battalion of incestuous males. Such was the fate of the Findlater castle, a sort of companion to Catherine's growing years. She'd come and look at it, tracing herself a path from the national school, feeding herself on Nestlé's chocolate, finding her hands growing sticky, rubbing them in daisies.

At school, Miss Rafter would recite the poetry of Yeats. 'Though I am old with wandering through hollow lands and hilly lands I will find out where she has gone.' Miss Rafter had pretty blonde hair, a lock of which fell from her forehead. She'd wear blouses as fine as a buttercup and her eyes always seemed shaking and about to flow with tears. Children stared at her, the few Protestant children of the locality. One day she left and years later Catherine saw her again, tempered by age but still lovely.

On going home Catherine would also hear about Yeats. Aunt Madeleine spoke freely on the subject. He used to visit the castle. He would dine there and speak about The Golden Dawn. In the 1930s, in Aunt Madeleine's youth, he would occasionally visit, push white hair from his forehead and recall his own youth and early temptresses as apple-blossom dipped from a bough. Aunt Madeleine would produce photographs in evidence of Yeats's visits. They hadn't been altogether clear but the white lain table on the lawn was in evidence, a shower of strawberries and a poet, leaning on a cane, staring into an unbeckoning afternoon.

Sometimes visitors would come, they also speaking of Yeats. A priest from a strange religion arrived in a long black dress and with a flowing beard. 'Russian Orthodox' was the name of the creed and Aunt Madeleine had expounded with him on the craft of Yeats. One or two visitors arrived from England. They spoke of the Queen. Aunt Madeleine had prepared a jelly dessert and they'd partaken of it, speaking of the Queen's imminent visit to New Zealand. That evening in bed Catherine had recourse to nightmare. She kept seeing her mother; her mother was running through the woods. Her mother was weeping. 'Mother.' She'd woken. She'd aired a slight tremor. She'd run down the stairs. She'd opened the kitchen door. She'd opened the drawing-room door. Inside was dark. Inside Aunt Madeleine was seated by the table, hands outstretched on the table, those of her visitors linking with hers and a candle lighting and a glass on the table, moving.

Her eyes opened once more.

She could hear a nurse saying, 'It will be a while yet.'

Her body slipped. Sleep now was kind; it flowed within her – like a river.

She understood no pain; all that was happening was happening from a force of persuasion. She had worked so hard for this moment, this moment when the past could be reckoned with and the present – for she knew it now – was the birth of a baby.

'Susan.' Madeleine had addressed her mother. She could still hear the voice of Madeleine cutting through the dark. 'Are you unhappy?' Catherine had conceived of that moment many times, a horrific crash, a scream, her scream. Madeleine had taken her and put her to bed. Sweat had oozed.

'Be easy, child,' Madeleine had said. 'Be easy.'

At the door the eyes of the English couple had stared, a point of fixation. They'd seemed so inane that Catherine had quietened, reflecting on the human race. She was ten now. She was growing up.

She'd run in the fields, she'd talked to sheep, she'd sit in the garden eating honey. She'd dance to the music of the gramophone as Aunt Madeleine typed an essay about Bucharest for some English newspaper.

Visitors were scarce now; Aunt Madeleine was drinking port and murmuring to herself and one summer's day in the garden she'd begun weeping as bees hummed about her. That had been one of the first of these flights. Many followed. Her lips were growing redder from port and her voice more cackly. A woman who'd been no more than a guardian for Catherine was emerging as a personality. The shock of seeing Madeleine talk to her mother had given way to curiosity. Catherine would stand at the top of the stairs as Aunt Madeleine recited poetry in a blue nightdress at the bottom. It was not poetry by Yeats but poetry by an obscure Rumanian poet about whom Aunt Madeleine had written a book.

Sometimes she'd cackle away in words of Rumanian, mixing them with remarks about wine, about bridges in Paris, about church railings in Trieste. Aunt Madeleine was becoming obsessed.

One day as the gramophone was playing *Tales from the Vienna Woods* Catherine had found Aunt Madeleine sleeping in a chair in the garden, port slipping from her mouth like blood.

The following winter Catherine had trailed to school. Aunt Madeleine was spending much of her time in bed. Catherine would make her cocoa and Aunt Madeleine would speak about the jackdaws outside. 'Such noisy creatures,' she'd remark, 'such noisy creatures.'

Catherine was now in the position of looking after Aunt Madeleine. Sometimes when Catherine entered her room she looked more like a man. One day Aunt Madeleine had risen from bed, put on her good clothes, brought Catherine to Dublin. They'd climbed Nelson's pillar, they'd munched a strawberry ice-cream in a café beside the bridge. They'd walked avenues sprouting with blossom. Both of them had sometimes stared, bewildered at the beauty of the city. Catherine was now twelve. Having seen enough films at the cinema in Carrick-on-Suir to have become acquainted with devious pasts she was now beginning to realize Aunt Madeleine had a divided history. That day on an avenue near Trinity College an old man with a white beard had called Madeleine. He'd come running towards her. He'd had gold in his white hair and a cap on his head. Madeleine had stared at him. Her eyes had been like frightened butterflies. 'Peter,' he'd kept saying. 'Peter.' Aunt Madeleine had kept babbling. She'd spoken of books, of a novel she had begun writing. Eventually she'd said 'I killed him. I know that.'

The train back to Wexford had taken them through countryside burning with spring. Aunt Madeleine had kept uttering under her breath, 'When all the wild summer was in her gaze.'

As summer approached she worked continuously on her

novel, seated by a table in the garden, a silk robe with an orange sun on the back flowing on her, her narrow fingers tapping the typewriter. One day her manuscript had flown away and she'd shrieked, pursuing the leaves until she had the last one, sodden in a pond where a water-lily was about to jump open.

A publisher had arrived from London, a newspaper man. There were photographs of Aunt Madeleine sitting on park benches in Trieste in the English Sunday papers. She had been rediscovered. Her years peeled away in the garden. There was a pink robe she wore that summer and tulips sprung like strangers. Catherine was now growing up in a world of the literary élite.

Madeleine's novel was a huge success. Others of her books were reprinted and one day in autumn some years later Catherine and Aunt Madeleine had packed their bags and left for London. Aunt Madeleine had been awarded a literary prize. Catherine had been grabbed from boarding school and with Aunt Madeleine she crossed the Irish sea. They'd landed in Wales, taken a train to London and there stayed in a house white as wedding cake in a square where leaves were falling, and Catherine bemoaned the fact she could not appear in *The White Horse Inn* at school.

She hadn't been away in boarding school long enough not to notice that behind the beautiful features which were reforming on Aunt Madeleine's face was fear. Sometimes on visits to the school those features had seemed blotched and awkward.

What was it Aunt Madeleine was seeking to hide? Where were the secrets? Catherine would have wandered the house demanding answers had she not had a fleeting fancy for a teacher at school who looked like Marianne Faithful.

To the house in the square had come men grown old before their time and women young in years but old in expression. London's literary world had convened. Catherine had attended the odd lesson given by a Rumanian in Bedford Square and returned to find pictures of Yeats on the wall and old men speaking of magic.

She had stopped outside the oak doorway to the living-room one day. 'Peter was a man of remarkable charm,' an old man was saying. 'He was one of the most remarkable poets of his time. Someday that shall be known.'

That evening Aunt Madeleine had stalked about; young men were coming to the house now. They were driving up in red sports cars and Aunt Madeleine was wearing mini-skirts. She'd had power over age. She was as one of the young models of London. She had been seeing a particular young man with hair like summer sunsets, gold and pale and partly blond. He'd been angelic. He'd worn red handkerchiefs in his pockets and occasionally a young woman telephoned, enquiring for him. Aunt Madeleine had taken him to her bedroom more than once. Once they'd screamed at one another. He'd left. Aunt Madeleine had stood on top of the stairs weeping. Catherine had touched her. 'We're going,' she'd said. 'We're going looking for him.'

In the following days Aunt Madeleine had swept along to Greek Orthodox churches, to Russian Orthodox churches. She'd lit candles before ikons. She'd whispered devotions. She'd summoned five older people to the house and performed a seance. This time Catherine had sat in the room next door reading a book by Hans Christian Andersen, realizing for the first time her aunt's all-out preoccupation with the dead. There'd been the seance with her mother when she'd been ten. There'd been the pictures of Isis among the teddy bears of childhood, there'd been chants her aunt had uttered, there'd been herbs she'd chosen on hills in midsummer. All this had been submerged in the stronger occultism of the area, crumbling castles, decaying teachers, whispering flowers.

Aunt Madeleine was now making no secret of it. Catherine had listened that evening. 'It's no good,' her aunt had said next door. Catherine had wandered through the house and picked up her aunt's book on the tarot, opened it on the hanged man, an illustration of a noose about a man's neck. 'The force of tribulation is in this card,' the commentary had

THE BIRTH OF LAUGHTER

read. Catherine had thumbed further through the book. Outside a wind was blowing up and she'd realized, page after page, that herein was contained a history. She'd been fifteen. She'd gone to the window, longed for Ireland, knew her life was beginning.

That evening Aunt Madeleine had announced, 'We're going to Europe.'

'Why?' Catherine had demanded. 'To seek him out?'

'He' was Peter. 'He' no longer was young men who called to the house or dapper princes with red limousines in London who took Aunt Madeleine out. 'He' was Aunt Madeleine's past.

Afterwards she would say to Adoe, what you grow up with you accept.

She'd accepted Aunt Madeleine, she'd lost herself in books, in primroses, in countryside. Now was the time, a sprightly fifteen-year-old she'd demanded questions, she'd asked herself the reason for Aunt Madeleine's extraordinary conglomeration of behaviour.

In later years she would meet young men in Dublin living-rooms who would quote Henry James to her. Certain quotations made sense. Quotations which indicated that there is a moment when personal search commences, search of roots, search of environment, search of past, present and sense of self.

She'd studied the reflection of her hair in a dark taxi which drove through London that evening, blonde on black, autumn outside, a penetrating chill in the leaves, in the faintness of light under a moonless sky.

They'd crossed to Ostend. 'Where are we going?' Catherine had asked. Her aunt had looked at her. She'd been wearing white. Her eyebrows had been defined in black. She'd looked at Catherine and as she had, Catherine had been astounded by the rocking of the ship. 'We're seeking him out. Haven't I told you?'

'Him.' Peter. That moment Catherine had assimilated all. There'd been a man. He'd ruined Madeleine's life. He'd haunted her.

They'd arrived in Brussels. It had been late at night. A shop had been open and they'd indulged in chips with mayonnaise on top. A woman with a kindly face had served them.

'I was in love,' Aunt Madeleine had said. 'I was in love. It was after my first book appeared. I was walking down Southampton Row one day with a rose on my dress when I saw him, I'd seen him in the newspaper the previous Sunday. I said hello. Peter was one of those people who emerge from nowhere. In the twenties there were many. G.I. Gurdjieff was one, men without backgrounds. Peter claimed to be Rumanian. I wrote about him as such. But he wrote in English. He had one of those faces that had registered wine, women, earthquakes, revolutions. He fell in love with me and I fell in love with him. We wrote to one another. We exchanged notes under chandeliers at crowded dinner parties. We confronted something in one another, what would you call it? That not easily defined substance, a soul. In Peter I saw the fruition of my youth, my work, my ability to write. He likewise saw such things in me.

'His work gravitated towards the very fine; there were whispers in his poetry of all kinds of occultism. From my background I was acquainted with the herbs of Wexford, the cards of the tarot, the cult of Isis. I'd spoken to Yeats of seances he'd observed in his youth and despite his warning I partook in the rites – at first but mildly then acquainting myself with the souls of the lonely, those who always came at will to the room wherein a seance is taking place. These were the things of my youth, certain potions for certain ailments, and a deck of cards that read the past as well as the future. But Peter's connections were more intimate with the supernatural. He'd discussed evocation of evil with dignitaries of a certain cult known to touch on a world of which many people were aware at the time, a world wherein were amassing forces of evil which were going to take over the world. These people wished to control these forces. Perhaps out of good, perhaps because of interest in power. Talk of power was everywhere, power over words, power over people.

'Peter and I journeyed up and down the east coast of Ireland; we stopped in houses where we partook of seances and spoke to dead elders. We travelled to Europe; 1936. The year Mussolini rode into Abyssinia I rode into the Mediterranean with Peter on a horse at Saintes Maries de la Mer in the south of France. It was in October, in honour of St Sarah, patroness of gipsies. We were on a voyage, in the heat of autumn we drank wine, smoked Turkish cigarettes; there were cracked mirrors in every little hotel but in our way we knew we were projecting elegance, that extraordinary quality only young people can project, a perfect image of life, a stability the wise can never know. There were bottles of red wine and young men in white suits. Europe was going to pieces but we travelled like patterns on wallpaper to Cairo; we, a poet and a young lady writer, were part of the effulgence of Europe before collapse. We were the cool flowers before the "blood-dimmed waters" rose. Such knowledge forced us to pray one day; in a church in Sardinia, the two of us on wooden pews.

'Going back on our path, however, we were drawn into knots of Peter's friends, those with contacts in Scotland, England, Ireland. At first our meetings with these people were friendly. Then they were otherwise. Partaking in a seance in Gibraltar I knew our mission was not holy, Peter's friends were trying to control the spiritual rather than allowing the spiritual to control them. They were delving into the interior of a spiritual landscape, a landscape born of evil. They were victims of a desire that surpassed sanity. They desired a say in a new ascendancy, an ascendancy of evil.

'How can I tell you why I became involved? I became involved out of love. I loved Peter. He loved me. He was more victim than I. He'd dabbled in something. It had become his life!'

Catherine had folded her nightdress carefully the following morning. She and Aunt Madeleine had let the light in. They'd boarded a train to Paris. It was to be the location. They were going to try to contact Peter.

'Love,' Aunt Madeleine had explained, 'is a strange thing. It occurs less frequently than we imagine. It is the most surprising and most nourishing thing in life. It is indeed holy. That is why I want to go back and contact Peter. I love him. When we arrived in Paris during the spring of 1937 Peter began thrusting himself into the company of a girl mixed up in his group. This group was making strange wooden instruments. They were preparing for a final evocation of the forces they'd attained to. I recognized waywardness in myself. Though not a Catholic I prayed at the Sacré Coeur. I knew he loved me. About me he'd written the finest of his poetry. Now this distortion was coming over him. He was leaving me to drink wine alone in a hotel, going off, making love to a Finnish girl. I forgave him twice. The third time I said I was leaving. It was in the hotel room. It was nearly June. There were roses, partly yellow, partly red. He seized them and stuck the thorns on his wrists until the red of his blood commingled with the red of the roses. I took a bag and made to go, stayed with him, made love, knew there couldn't be anything in my life more holy than this.

'I awoke with him in the late evening to dreams of flowering trees in Wexford. We walked by the Seine. We knew we were utterly, utterly in love. Yet it was as though there was a wall in front of us. I said I was leaving the group. There was almost a grotesque look on Peter's face. He continued going to their meetings. He did not see the Finnish girl. I was writing a novel. One day he did not come back. He stayed away three days. I wished to kill myself, not out of love for him but because I knew there'd be no other love. He returned. I knew he'd been with the girl. It was drawing near expiration time for his group. They were about to summon the forces of – of the Anti-Christ. I said goodbye to him. I walked to Gard du Nord. Here, suitcase in my hand before boarding the train, I wished him dead.

'Peter's body was found in a small hotel which had burnt down some days later. There were roses outside, I saw by the newspaper photographs. I returned to Ireland. I told my friends who were Peter's friends I had killed him, but they said his death was an atonement, that the time had not yet come for the intended resurrection of the powers of evil, that there was still time to go. That time I suppose came with the first bombs on Notting Hill Gate. I became like a ghost during these years. I became unhappy and yet knew that my unhappiness was a source of possible reparation. I wished to speak to Peter again. There was no card in the tarot which would speak of him. And I had only myself to talk to. In time I held parties. Young men came to them and one called Alec I fell in love with. We went to Paris together. I conceived his child. The child was born mongoloid and died. I knew I should not have returned to this city. I went back to Wexford and there raised you, Catherine. There were times I made to speak to Peter. I could not contact him. In Paris now I know he will come. It is best I speak to the dead.'

She should have known the unholiness of the mission. Yet Aunt Madeleine had convinced her of the exigencies of their affair, an affair which hung half-way between God and the devil, an affair which included into its substance fat roses on spring days in Paris in the temporal haze before the war. 'I know,' Aunt Madeleine had said, 'that life is short. There are certain things within one's life one must guard like new unopened roses. Such was my affair with Peter. It was all such a terrible mistake, our dabbling in this magic. The young are wont to make mistakes. It seems like a dream now, the purpose of our seances in Gibraltar and Paris. But the real nightmare was in the human heart, the heart which couldn't distinguish and protect love when it had arrived.'

In Paris they'd made tracks to the house of a Russian woman whom Aunt Madeleine had conversed with. It had occurred to Catherine that they were partaking in more than a backward journey, this was the journey of a soul towards the point of its possession. She'd chosen cards from the tarot in the following days. Always the card of the hanged man had attained the most prominent place.

In their little hotel Catherine had studied Yeats, had read

her aunt's novels and knew there were times in history that were irrevocably evil – such a time was her aunt's time. Aunt Madeleine unknowingly had slipped into dimensions of evil through an innocent affair, and the unfortunate succumbing to things supernatural, things dangerous.

Aunt Madeleine had arranged a seance with the Russian woman as medium. All the time the prominence of youth seemed to ride on her face. Catherine had been frightened. She'd warned her aunt against it, her aunt had insisted. They'd entered a dark room. She needn't have partaken if she hadn't so desired but something in her had insisted. She'd desired to know the darkness of her roots, and the inability of extraordinary and innocent people like Aunt Madeleine to cope with their fates.

The baby was coming. It was pushing forward. Catherine's eyes opened. She thrilled to see Adoe knowing her last sight òf him had been in the garden before the baby had begun. His eyes sparkled, ingrained with copper points. She made to reach him, then saw Peter's face as she'd encountered it at that seance in Paris, collapsed writhing, screaming, until the density of hell seemed to burst from her.

Afterwards she'd struggled to know about such phenomena. In some seances it is reported that the medium can take the shape of the spirit she aspires to communicate with. This is called an ectoplasm. That evening in Paris such a strangeness had occurred. The Russian woman's face had transformed into Peter's ashen resemblance.

How much of what Aunt Madeleine had told her was true she'd never know. All she'd known was that Aunt Madeleine's involvement in evil had been greater than she'd admitted; love there may have been between her and Peter but her involvement in the group had been greater than she'd explained.

She'd been a high-priestess in this unfortunate cult. She'd cursed Peter when he'd sought to escape it.

She'd returned to Ireland on his death. Ever since she'd tried to build a shrine of images, of actions to him in order to reach him again. These images, those actions had accumulated in that ghastly seance in Paris when Catherine had screamed and her aunt had shot out of the door, hollering 'I'm evil. I'm evil. I'm evil.'

The truth had emerged, laden with the horror of its homecoming. The ancestral castle had been the starting point in a European cult to aggravate the forces of evil, provoke them to a point of emergence whereby they could be harnessed. This plot was known to few and poets like Yeats and young statesmen had visited the castle, knowing only its jovial side and the effulgence of its roses.

Catherine had never walked its paths again until she'd returned with Adoe. The facts about Aunt Madeleine she'd picked up in a witch hunt among Dublin elders. Aunt Madeleine had been incapacitated since that evening in Paris. When Catherine had taken an overdose of weed-killer in her final year at school Aunt Madeleine had visited her in hospital, an ashen effigy. When she'd fallen in with a theatre group in Dublin to whom Adoe had belonged, Aunt Madeleine had appeared, strictly forbidding her against men and especially those involved in theatre. 'They bring wounds,' she'd said, 'they bring your downfall.'

They'd been sitting in one of Bewleys oriental cafés when Catherine had noticed the tears in Aunt Madeleine's eyes and knew her to have repented. She'd been in love once. Wasn't that all you could judge her on? Peter had fallen in love with another woman, a Finnish girl belonging to a circus who had tried to persuade him away from a world of spirits, incantations and words about an apocalypse.

There had been an old man sitting behind Aunt Madeleine. Catherine had asked herself, 'How can I know about a generation other than my own? Above all how can I judge its torments, its fears, its movements – its indulgences?'

She'd been playing the young girl in *A Month in the Country*, her first main role, when she'd learnt Aunt Madeleine had died. It had been the time when yellow tulips would be nosing themselves unsuccessfully around the castle walls. Aunt Madeleine had passed away in her cottage. The funeral had taken place in Dublin. It had been a May day, a day of flowering horse-chestnuts, a day of sunshine. Men of state had gathered, old men, ikons of Irish history. Catherine had wondered, perceiving the few men of literature, the men of state, how close to respectability and respectable quarters Aunt Madeleine's divinations had come?

An elderly gentleman with a beard turned to gold by acute rays of sunshine had read an oration. The puzzle was over. Catherine had turned away from the grave, the past was buried, save for the few intimations old men gave her of Aunt Madeleine's involvement or the questions asked of her by theatre people who presumed her to be an expert in the tarot.

Her eyes grazed with sunshine. She awoke. In front of her Adoe stood, he was holding a child. The child had his circuitous brown eyes. He bent, kissed her. She slept. This time her sleep was easier and her dreams wound with them a trail of January snowdrops, a smile of Aunt Madeleine, one of those extraordinary smiles she gave when she'd made a sponge cake, iced it with caramel and recalled the vibrancy, the possibilities of being young, raven-haired and a woman of talent, of 'exceptional talent' as the blurbs read and the old men stuttered, over whiskeys, at literary parties or on the streets of Dublin, Paris, London a long time ago when fogs descended more easily and circumstances always seemed to point to a world, somewhere beyond our own.

Jimmy

Her office overlooked the college grounds; early in the spring they were bedecked with crocuses and snowdrops. Looking down upon them was to excel oneself. She was a fat lady, known as 'Windy' by the students, her body heaved into sedate clothes and her eyes somehow always searching despite the student jibes that she was profoundly stupid and profoundly academic.

She lectured in ancient Irish history, yearly bringing students to view Celtic crosses and round towers marooned in spring floods. The college authorities often joined her on these trips, one administrator who insisted on speaking in Irish all the time. This was a college situated near Connemara, the Gaelic speaking part of Ireland. Irish was a big part of the curriculum; bespectacled, pioneer-pin-bearing administrators insisted on speaking Irish as though it was the tongue of foolish crows. There was an element of mindlessness about it. One spoke Irish because a state that had been both severe and regimental on its citizens had encouraged it.

Emily delayed by the window this morning. It was spring and foolishly she remembered the words of the blind poet Raftery: 'Now that it's spring the days will be getting longer. And after the feast of Brigid I'll set foot to the roads.' There was that atmosphere of instinct abroad in Galway today. Galway as long as she recalled was a city of travelling people, red-petticoated tinkers, clay-pipe-smoking sailors, wandering beggars.

In Eyre Square sat an austere statue of Padraic O Conaire,

an Irish scribe who'd once walked to Moscow to visit Chekhov and found him gone for the weekend.

In five minutes she would lecture on Brigid's crosses, the straw symbols of renewal in Ireland.

There was now evidence that Brigid was a lecher, a Celtic whore who was ascribed to sainthood by those who had slept with her but that altered nothing. She was one of the cardinal Irish holy figures, the Isis of the spring-enchanted island.

Emily put words together in her mind.

In five minutes they'd confront her, pleased faces pushing forward. These young people had been to New York or Boston for their summer holidays. They knew everything that was to be known. They sneered a lot, they smiled little. They were possessed of good looks, spent most of the day lounging in the Cellar bar, watching strangers, for even students had the wayward Galway habit of eyeing a stranger closely, for it was a city tucked away in a corner of Ireland, peaceable, prosperous, seaward-looking.

After class that day she returned to the college canteen where she considered the subject of white sleeveless jerseys. Jimmy used to have one of those. They'd gone to college in the 1930s, Earlsfort Terrace in Dublin and Jimmy used to wear one of those jerseys. They'd sit in the dark corridor, a boy and a girl from Galway, pleased that the trees were again in bloom, quick to these things by virtue of coming from Galway where nature dazzled.

Their home was outside Galway city, six miles from it, a big house, an elm tree on either side of it and in spring two pools of snowdrops like hankies in front of it.

Jimmy had gone to Dublin to study English literature. She had followed him in a year to study history. They were respectable children of a much lauded solicitor and they approached their lives gently. She got a job in the university in Galway. He got a job teaching in Galway city.

Mrs Carmichael, lecturer in English, approached.

Mrs Carmichael wore her grandmother's Edwardian clothes

because though sixty, she considered it in keeping with what folk were wearing in Carnaby Street in London.

'Emily, I had trouble today,' she confessed. 'A youngster bit a girl in class.'

Emily smiled, half from chagrin, half from genuine amusement.

Mrs Carmichael was a bit on the Anglo-Irish side, taut, upper-class, looking on these Catholic students as one might upon a rare and rather charming breed of radishes.

'Well, tell them to behave themselves,' Emily said. 'That's what I always say.'

She knew from long experience that they did not obey, that they laughed at her and that her obesity was hallmarked by a number of nicknames. She could not help it, she ate a lot, she enjoyed cakes in Lydons' and more particularly when she went to Dublin she enjoyed Bewley's and country-shop cakes.

In fact the country-shop afforded her not just a good pot of tea and nice ruffled cream cakes but a view of the green, a sense again of student days, here in Dublin, civilized, parochial. She recalled the woman with the oval face who became famous for writing stories and the drunkard who wrote strange books that now young people read.

'I'll see you tomorrow,' Mrs Carmichael said, leaving.

Emily watched her. She'd sail in her Anglia to her house in the country, fleeing this uncivilized mess.

Emily put her handkerchief into her handbag and strolled home.

What was it about this spring? Since early in the year strange notions had been entering her head. She'd been half-thinking of leaving for Paris for a few days or spending a weekend in West Cork.

There was both desire and remembrance in the spring.

In her parents' home her sister, Sheila, now lived. She was married. Her husband was a vet.

Her younger brother, George, was working with the European Economic Community in Brussels.

Jimmy alone was unheard of, unlisted in conversation.

He'd gone many years ago, disappearing on a mail train when the war was waging in the outside world. He'd never come back; some said he was an alcoholic on the streets of London. If that were so he'd be an eloquent drunkard. He had so much, Jimmy had, so much of his race, astuteness, learning, eyes that danced like Galway Bay on mornings when the islands were clear and when gulls sparkled like flecks of foam.

She considered her looks, her apartment, sat down, drank tea. It was already afternoon and the Dublin train hooted, shunting off to arrive in Dublin in the late afternoon.

Tom, her brother-in-law, always said Jimmy was a moral retrograde, to be banished from mind. Sheila always said Jimmy was better off gone. He was too confused in himself. George, the youngest of the family, recalled only that he'd read him Oscar Wilde's *The Happy Prince* once and that tears had broken down his cheeks.

The almond blossom had not yet come and the war trembled in England and in a month Jimmy was gone and his parents were glad. Jimmy had been both a nuisance and a scandal. Jimmy had let the family down.

Emily postured over books on Celtic mythology, taking notes.

It had been an old custom in Ireland to drive at least one of your family out, to England, to the mental hospital, to sea or to a bad marriage. Jimmy had not fallen easily into his category. He'd been a learned person, a very literate young man. He'd taught in a big school, befriended a young man, the 1930s prototype with blond hair, went to Dublin one weekend with him, stayed in Buswells Hotel with him, was since branded by names they'd put on Oscar Wilde. Jimmy had insisted on his innocence but the boy lied before going to Dublin, telling his parents that he was going to play a hurling match.

Jimmy had to resign his job; he took to drink, he was banished from home, slipping in in the afternoons to read to

George. Eventually he'd gone. The train had registered nothing of his departure as it whinnied in the afternoon. He just slipped away.

The boy, Johnny Fogarthy, whom Jimmy had abducted to Dublin, himself left Ireland.

He went to the States, ended up in the antique trade and in 1949, not yet twenty-seven, was killed in Pacifica. Local mind construed all elements of this affair to be tragic.

Jimmy was safely gone.

The dances at the crossroads near their home ceased and that was the final memory of Jimmy, dancing with a middle-aged woman and she wearing earrings and an accordion bleating 'The Valley of Slievenamban'.

Emily heard a knock on the door early next morning. Unrushed she went to the door. She was wearing a pink gown. Her hair was in a net. She had been expecting no caller but then again the postman knocked when he had a parcel.

For years afterwards she would tell people of the thoughts that had been haunting her mind in the days previously.

She opened the door.

A man aged but not bowed by age, derelict but not disarrayed, stood outside.

There was a speed in her eyes which detected the form of a man older than Jimmy her brother but yet holding his features and hiding nothing of the graciousness of which he was possessed.

She held him. He held her. There was anguish in her eyes. Her fat hands touched an old man.

'Jimmy,' she said simply.

Jimmy the tramp had won £100 at the horses and chosen from a variety of possibilities a home-visit. Jimmy the tramp lived on Charing Cross Road.

Jimmy the tramp was a wino, yes, but like many of his counterparts near St-Martin-in-the Fields in London was an eloquent one. Simply Jimmy was home.

News brushed swiftly to the country. His brother-in-law

reared. His sister, Sheila, silenced. Emily, in her simple way, was overjoyed.

News was relayed to Brussels. George, the younger brother, was expected home in two weeks.

That morning Emily led Jimmy to a table, laid it as her own mother would have done ceremoniously with breakfast things and near a pitcher, blue and white, they prayed.

Emily's prayer was one of thanksgiving.

Jimmy's too was one of thanksgiving.

Emily poured milk over porridge and dolled the porridge with honey from Russia, invoking for Jimmy the time Padraic O Conaire walked to Moscow.

In the afternoon he dressed in clothes Emily bought for him and they walked the streets of Galway. Jimmy by the Claddagh, filled as it was with swans, wept the tears of a frail human being.

'Emily,' he said. 'This should be years ago.'

For record he said there'd been no interest other than platonic in the young boy, that he'd been wronged and this wrong had driven him to drink. 'I hope you don't think I'm apologizing,' he said, 'I'm stating facts.'

Sheila met him and Tom, his brother-in-law, who looked at him as though at an animal in the zoo.

Emily had prepared a meal the first evening of his return. They ate veal, drank rosé d'Anjou, toasted by a triad of candles. 'One for love, one for luck, one for happiness,' indicated Emily.

Tom said the EEC made things good for farmers, bad for businessmen. Sheila said she was going to Dublin for a hairdo.

Emily said she'd like to bring Jimmy to the old house next day.

Sure enough the snowdrops were there when they arrived and the frail trees.

Jimmy said as though in speed he'd lived as a tramp for years, drinking wine, beating his breast in pity.

'It was all an illusion,' he said. 'This house still stands.'

He entered it, a child, and Tom, his brother-in-law, looked scared.

Jimmy went to the library and sure enough the works of Oscar Wilde were there.

'Many a time *The Happy Prince* kept me alive,' he said.

Emily dressed newly, her dignity cut a hole in her pupils. They silenced and listened to talk about Romanesque doorways.

She lit her days with thoughts of the past, rooms not desecrated, appointments under the elms.

Her figure cut through Galway. Spring came in a rush. There was no dalliance. The air shattered with freshness.

As she lectured Jimmy walked. He walked by the Claddagh, by Shop Street, by Quay Street. He looked, he pondered, his gaze drifted to Clare.

Once Johnny Fogarthy had told him he was leaving for California on the completion of his studies. He left all right.

He was killed.

'For love,' Jimmy told Emily. He sacrificed himself for the speed of a car on the Pacific coast.

They dined together and listened to Bach. Tom and Sheila kept away.

Emily informed Jimmy about her problems. Jimmy was wakeful to them. In new clothes, washed, he was the aged poet, distinguished, alert to the unusual, the charming, the indirect.

'I lived in a world of craftsmen,' he told Emily, 'most alcoholics living on the streets are poets driven from poetry, lovers driven from their beloved, craftsmen exiled from their craft.'

They assuaged those words with drink.

Emily held Jimmy's hand. 'I hope you are glad to be here,' she said.

'I am, I am,' he said.

The weekend in Dublin with Johnny Fogarthy he'd partaken of spring lamb with him on a white lain table in Buswell's he told Emily.

'We drank wine then too, rosé, age made no difference between us. We were elucidated by friendship, its acts, its meaning. Pity love was mistaken for sin.'

Jimmy had gone during the war and he told Emily about the bombs, the emergencies, the crowded air-raid shelters.

'London was on fire. But I'd have chosen anything, anything to the gap in people's understanding in Ireland.'

They drank to that.

Emily at college was noted now for a new beauty.

Jimmy in his days walked the streets.

Mrs Kenny in Kenny's bookshop recognized him and welcomed him. Around were writers' photographs on the wall. 'It's good to see you,' she said.

He had represented order once, white sleeveless jumpers, fairish hair evenly parted, slender volumes of English poetry.

'Remember,' Mrs Kenny said, 'the day O'Duffy sailed to Spain with the blueshirts and you, a boy, said they should be beaten with their own rosary beads.'

They laughed.

Jimmy had come home not as an aged tramp but as a poet. It could not have been more simple if he'd come from Cambridge, a retired don. Those who respected the order in him did not seek undue information. Those puzzled by him demanded all the reasons.

Those like Tom, his brother-in-law, who hated him, resented his presence. 'I sat here once with Johnny,' Jimmy told Emily one day on the Connemara coast. 'He said he needed something from life, something Ireland could not give him. So he went to the States.'

'Wise man.'

'But he was killed.'

'We were the generation expecting early and lucid deaths,' he told Emily.

Yes. But Jimmy's death had been his parents' mortification with him, his friends' disavowal of him, Emily's silence in her eyes. He'd gone, dispirited, rejected. He'd gone, someone who'd deserted his own agony.

'You're back,' Emily said to him cheerily. 'That's the most important thing.'

His brother, George, came back from Brussels, a burly man in his forties.

He was cheerful and gangly at encountering Jimmy. He recognized integrity, recalled Jimmy reading him *The Happy Prince*, embraced the old man.

Over gin in Emily's he said, 'The EEC is like everything else, boring. You'll be bored in Tokyo, bored in Brussels, bored in Dublin.' Emily saw that Jimmy was not bored.

In the days he walked through town, wondering at change, unable to account for it, the new buildings, the supermarkets. His hands were held behind his back. Emily often watched him, knowing that like de Valera he represented something of Ireland. But an element other than pain, fear, loneliness. He was the artist. He was the one foregone and left out in a rush to be acceptable.

They attended mass in the pro-cathedral. Jimmy knelt, prayed; Emily wondered, were his prayers sincere? She looked at Christ, situated quite near the mosaic of President Kennedy, asked him to leave Jimmy, for him not to return. She enjoyed his company as though that of an erstwhile lover.

Sheila threw a party one night.

The reasoning that led to this event was circumspect. George was home. He did not come home often. And when he did he stayed only a few days.

It was spring. The house had been spring-cleaned. A new carpet now graced the floor. Blossom threatened; lace divided the carpet with its shadows.

All good reasons to entertain the local populace.

But deep in Sheila, that aggravated woman's mind, must have been the knowledge that Jimmy, being home, despite his exclusion from all ceremony, despite his rather nebulous circumstances, his homecoming had by some decree to be both established and celebrated.

So neighbours were asked, those who'd borne rumour of him once, those who rejected him and yet were only too willing to accept his legend, young teacher in love with blond boy, affair discovered, young teacher flees to the gutters of London, blond boy ends up in a head-on collision in Pacifica, a town at the toe of San Francisco, California.

The first thing Jimmy noticed was a woman singing 'I have seen the lark soar high at morn' next to a sombre ancient piano.

Emily had driven him from Galway, she beside him in a once-a-lifetime cape saw his eyes and the shadow that crossed them. He was back in a place which had rejected him. He had returned, bearing no triumph but his own humility.

Emily chatted to Mrs Connaire and Mrs Delaney. To them, though a spinster, she was a highly erudite member of the community and as such acknowledged by her peers.

Emily looked about. Jimmy was gone. She thrust herself through the crowd and discovered Jimmy after making her way up a stairway hung with paintings of cattle-marts and islands, in a room by himself, the room in which he had once slept.

'Jimmy.' He turned.

'Yes.'

'Come down.'

Like a lamb he conceded.

They walked again into the room where a girl aged seventeen sang 'The leaving of Liverpool'.

It was a party in the old style with pots of tea and whiskey and slender elegant cups.

George said, 'It's great to see the country changing, isn't it? It's great to see people happy.'

Emily thought of the miles of suburban horror outside Galway and thought otherwise.

Tom slapped Jimmy's back. Tom, it must be stated, did not desire this party, not at least until Jimmy was gone. His wife's intentions he suspected but he let it go ahead.

'It's great having you,' he said to Jimmy, bitter and sneering from drink. 'Isn't it you that was the queer fellow throwing up a good job for a young lad?'

Emily saw the pain, sharp, smitten, like an arrow.

She would have reached for him as she would have for a child smitten by a bomb in the North of Ireland but the crowd churned and he was lost from sight.

Tom sang 'If I had a hammer'. Sheila, plagued by the social success of her party, wearing earrings like toadstools, sang 'I left my heart in San Francisco'.

A priest who'd eyed Jimmy but had not approached him sang 'Lullaby on Broadway'.

George, Jimmy's young brother working in the EEC, got steadily drunker. Tom was slapping the precocious backsides of young women. Sheila was dancing attendance with cucumber sandwiches.

Jimmy was talking to a blond boy whom, if you stretched memory greatly, resembled Johnny Fogarthy.

The fire blazed.

Their parents might have turned in their grave, hating Jimmy their child because he was the best of their brood and sank the lowest.

Emily sipped sherry and talked to neighbours about cows and sheep and daughters with degrees in medicine and foreign countries visited.

She saw her brother and mentally adjusted his portrait, he was again a young man very handsome, if you like, in love in an idle way with one of his pupils.

In love in a way one person gives to another a secret, a share in their happiness.

She would have stopped all that was going to happen to him but knew that she couldn't.

Tom, her brother-in-law, was getting drunker and viler.

He said out loud, 'What is it that attracts men to young fellows?' surprising Jimmy in a simple conversation with a blond boy.

The party ceased, music ceased. All looked towards Jimmy, looked away. The boy was Mrs McDonagh's son, going from one pottery to another in Ireland to learn his trade, never satisfied, always moving, recently taken up with the Divine light, some religious crowd in Galway.

People stared. The image was authentic. There was not much sin in it but a lot of beauty. They did not share Tom's prejudice but left the man and the boy. It was getting late. The country was changing and if there had been wounds why couldn't they be forgotten?

Tom was slobbering. His wife attended him. He was slobbering about Jimmy, always afraid of that element of his wife's family, always afraid strange children would be born to him but none came anyway. His wife brought him to the toilet where presumably he got sick.

George, drunk on gin, talked about the backsides of secretaries in Brussels and Jimmy, alone among the crowd, still eloquent with drink, spoke to the blond teenager about circuses long ago.

'Why did you leave Ireland?' the boy asked him.

'Searching,' he said, 'searching for something. Why did you leave your last job?'

'Because I wasn't satisfied,' the boy said. 'You've got to go on, haven't you? There's always that sense that there's more than this.'

The night was rounded by a middle-aged woman who'd once met Count John McCormack singing 'Believe me if all those endearing young charms'.

On the way back into Galway Emily felt revered and touched by time, recalled Jimmy, his laughter once, that laughter more subdued now.

She was glad he was back, glad of his company and despite everything clear in her mind that the past was a fantasy. People had needed culprits then, people had needed fallen angels.

She said goodnight to Jimmy, touched him on the cheek with a kiss.

'See you in the morning,' she said.

She didn't.

She left him asleep, made tea for herself, contemplated the spring sky outside.

She went to college, lectured on Celtic crosses, lunched

with Mrs Carmichael, drove home in the evening, passing the sea, the Dublin train sounding distantly in her head. The party last night had left a strange colour inside her, like light in wine or a reflection on a saxophone.

What was it that haunted her about it, she asked herself? Then she knew.

She remembered Jimmy on a rain-drenched night during the war coming to the house and his parents turning him away.

Why was it Sheila had thrown the party? Because she had to requite the spirit of the house.

Why was it Jimmy had come back to the house? Because he needed to reassert himself to the old spirits there.

Why was it she was glad? Because her brother was home and at last she had company to glide into old age.

She opened the door. Light fell, guiltily.

Inside was a note.

'Took the Dublin train. Thanks for everything. Love Jimmy.'

The note closed in her hand like a building falling beneath a bomb and the scream inside her would have dragged her into immobility had not she noticed the sky outside, golden, futuristic, the colour of the sky over their home when Easter was near and she a girl in white, not fat, beautiful even, walked with her brother, a boy in a sleeveless white jersey, by a garden drilled in daffodils, expecting nothing less than the best life could offer.

Memories of Swinging London

Why he went there he did not know, an instinctive feel for a dull façade, an intuition born out of time of a country unbeknownst to him now but ten years ago one of excessive rain, old stone damaged by time and trees too green, too full.

He was drunk, of course, the night he stumbled in there at ten o'clock. It had been three weeks since Marion had left him, three weeks of drink, of moronic depression, three weeks of titillating jokes with the boys at work.

Besides it had been raining that night and he'd needed shelter.

She was tired after a night's drama class when he met her, a small nun making tea with a brown kettle.

Her garb was grey and short and she spoke with a distinctive Kerry accent but yet a polish at variance with her accent.

She'd obviously been to an elocution class or two, Liam thought cynically, until he perceived her face, weary, alone, a makeshift expression of pain on it.

She'd failed that evening with her lesson, she said. Nothing had happened, a half dozen boys from Roscommon and Leitrim had left the hall uninspired.

Then she looked at Liam as though wondering who she was speaking to anyway, an Irish drunk, albeit a well-dressed one. In fact he was particularly well-dressed that evening, wearing a neatly cut grey suit and a white shirt, spotless but for some dots of Guinness.

They talked with some reassurance when he was less drunk. He sat back as she poured tea.

She was from Kerry she said, West Kerry. She'd been a few months in Africa and a few months in the United States but this was her first real assignment, other than a while as domestic science teacher in a Kerry convent. Here she was all of nurse, domestic and teacher. She taught young men from Mayo and Roscommon how to move; she had become keen on drama while going to college in Dublin. She'd pursued this interest while teaching domestic science in Kerry, an occupation she was ill-qualified for, having studied English literature in Dublin.

'I'm a kind of social worker,' she said, 'I'm given these lads to work with. They come here looking for something. I give them drama.'

She'd directed Eugene O'Neill in West Kerry, she'd directed Arthur Miller in West Kerry. She'd moulded young men there but a different kind of young men, bank clerks. Here she was landed with labourers, drunks.

'How did you come by this job?' Liam asked.

She looked at him, puzzled by his directness.

'They were looking for a suitable spot to put an ardent Sister of Mercy,' she said.

There was a lemon iced cake in a corner of the room and she caught his eye spying it and she asked him if he'd like some, apologizing for not offering him some earlier. She made quite a ceremony of cutting it, dishing it up on a blue-rimmed plate.

He picked at it.

'And you,' she said, 'what part of Ireland do you come from?'

He had to think about it for a moment. It had been so long. How could he tell her about limestone streets and dank trees? How could he convince her he wasn't lying when he spun yarns about an adolescence long gone?

'I come from Galway,' he said, 'from Ballinasloe.'

'My father used to go to the horse fair there,' she said. And then she was off again about Kerry and farms, until suddenly she realized it should be him that should be speaking.

She looked at him but he said nothing.

He was peaceful. He had a cup of tea, a little bit of lemon cake left.

'How long have you been here?' she asked.

'Ten years.'

He was unforthcoming with answers.

The aftermath of drink had left his body and he was sitting as he had not sat for weeks, consuming tea, peaceful. In fact, when he thought of it, he hadn't been like this for years, sitting quietly, untortured by memories of Ireland but easy with them, memories of green and limestone grey.

She invited him back and he didn't come back for days. But as always in the case of two people who meet and genuinely like one another they were destined to meet again.

He saw her in Camden Town one evening, knew that his proclivity to Keats and Byron at school was somehow justified. She was unrushed, carrying vegetables, asked him why he had not come. He told her he'd been intending to come, that he was going to come. She smiled. She had to go she said. She was firm.

Afterwards he drank, one pint of Guinness. He would go back he told himself.

In fact it was as though he was led by some force of persuasion, easiness of language which existed between him and Sister Sarah, a lack of embarrassment at silence.

He took a bus from his part of Shepherd's Bush to Camden Town. Rain slashed, knifing the evening with black. The first instinct he had was to get a return bus but unnerved he went on.

Entering the centre the atmosphere was suddenly appropriated by music, Tchaikovsky, *Swan Lake*. He entered the hall to see a half dozen young men in black jerseys, blue trousers, dying, quite genuinely like swans.

She saw him. He saw her. She didn't stop the procedure, merely acknowledged him and went on, her voice reverberating in the hall, to talk of movement, of the necessity to identify the real lines in one's body and flow with them.

Yes, he'd always recall that, 'The real lines in one's body.' When she had stopped talking she approached him. He stood there, aware that he was a stranger, not in a black jersey.

Then she wound up the night's procedure with more music, this time Beethoven, and the young men from Roscommon and Mayo behaved like constrained ballerinas as they simulated dusk.

Afterwards they spoke again. In the little kitchen.

'Dusk is a word for balance between night and day,' she said. 'I asked them to be relaxed, to be aware of time flowing through them.'

The little nun had an errand to make.

Alone, there, Liam smoked a cigarette. He thought of Marion, his wife gone north to Leeds, fatigued with him, with marriage, with the odd affair. She had worked as a receptionist in a theatre.

She'd given up her job, gone home to Mummy, left the big city for the northern smoke. In short her marriage had ended.

Looking at the litter-bin Liam realized how much closer to accepting this fact he'd come. Somehow he'd once thought marriage to be for life but here it was, one marriage dissolved and nights to fill, a body to shelter, a life to lead.

A young man with curly blond hair entered. He was looking for Sister Sarah. He stopped when he saw Liam, taken aback. These boys were like a special battalion of guards in their black jerseys. He was an intruder, cool, English almost, his face, his features relaxed, not rough or ruddy. The young man said he was from Roscommon. That was near Liam's home.

He spoke of farms, of pigs, said he'd had to leave, come to the city, search for neon. Now he'd found it. He'd never go back to the country. He was happy here, big city, many people, a dirty river and a population of people which included all races.

'I miss the dances though,' the boy said, 'the dances of Sunday nights. There's nothing like them in London, the cars

114

all pulled up and the ballroom jiving with music by Big Tom and the Mainliners. You miss them in London but there are other things that compensate.'

When asked by Liam what compensated most for the loss of fresh Sunday night dancehalls amid green fields the boy said, 'The freedom.'

Sister Sarah entered, smiled at the boy, sat down with Liam. The boy questioned her about a play they were intending to do and left, turning around to smile at Liam.

Sarah – her name came to him without the prefix now – spoke about the necessity of drama in schools, in education.

'It is a liberating force,' she said. 'It brings out – ' she paused ' – the swallow in people.'

And they both laughed, amused and gratified at the absurdity of the description.

Afterwards he perceived her in a hallway alone, a nun in a short outfit, considering the after-effects of her words that evening, pausing before plunging the place into darkness.

He told her he would return and this time he did, sitting among boys from Roscommon and Tipperary, improvising situations. She called on him to be a soldier returning from war and this he did, embarrassedly, recalling that he too was a soldier once, a boy outside a barracks in Ireland, beside a bed of crocuses. People smiled at his shattered innocence, at this attempt at improvisation. Sister Sarah reserved a smile. In the middle of a simulated march he stopped.

'I can't. I can't,' he said.

People smiled, let him be.

He walked to the bus stop, alone. Rain was edging him in, winter was coming. It hurt with its severity tonight. He passed a sex shop, neon light dancing over the instruments in the window. The pornographic smile of a British comedian looked out from a newsagent's.

He got his bus.

Sleep took him in Shepherd's Bush. He dreamt of a school long ago in County Galway which he attended for a few years, urns standing about the remains of a Georgian past.

At work people noticed he was changing. They noticed a greater serenity. An easiness about the way he was holding a cup. They virtually chastised him for it.

Martha McPherson looked at him, said sarcastically, 'You look hopeful.'

He was thinking of Keats in the canteen when she spoke to him, of words long ago, phrases from mouldering books at school at the beginning of autumn.

His flat was tidier now; there was a space for books which had not hitherto been there. He began a letter home, stopped, couldn't envisage his mother, old woman by a sea of bog.

Sister Sarah announced plans for a play they would perform at Christmas. The play would be improvised, bit by bit, and she asked for suggestions about the content.

One boy from Leitrim said, 'Let's have a play about the tinkers.'

Liam was cast for a part as tinker king and bit by bit over the weeks he tried, tried to push off shyness, act out little scenes.

People laughed at him. He felt humiliated, twisted inside. Yet he went on.

His face was moulding, clearer than before, and in his eyes was a piercing darkness,. He made speeches, trying to recall the way the tinkers spoke at home, long lines of them on winter evenings, camps in country lanes, smoke rising as a sun set over distant steeples.

He spoke less to colleagues, more to himself, phrasing and rephrasing old questions, wondering why he had left Ireland in the first place, a boy, sixteen, lonely, very lonely on a boat making its way through a winter night.

'I suppose I left Ireland,' he told Sister Sarah one night, 'because I felt ineffectual, totally ineffectual. The priests at school despised my independence. My mother worked as a char. My father was dead. I was a mature youngster who liked women, had one friend at school, a boy who wrote poetry.

'I came to England seeking reasons for living. I stayed with my older brother who worked in a factory.

'My first week in England a Greek homosexual who lived upstairs asked me to sleep with him. That ended my innocence. I grew up somewhere around then, became adult very, very young.'

1966, the year he left Ireland.

Sonny and Cher sang 'I've got you, babe'.

London was readying itself for blossoming, the Swinging Sixties had attuned themselves to Carnaby Street, to discothèques, to parks. Ties looked like huge flowers, young hippies sat in parks. And in 1967, the year 'Sergeant Pepper's Lonely Hearts Club Band' appeared, a generation of young men and horned-rimmed glasses looking like John Lennon. 'It was like a party,' Liam said, 'a continual party. I ate, drank at this feast.

'Then I met Marion. We married in 1969, the year Brian Jones died. I suppose we spent our honeymoon at his funeral. Or at least in Hyde Park where Mick Jagger read a poem in commemoration of him. "Weep no more for Adonais is not dead." '

Sister Sarah smiled. She obviously liked romantic poetry too, she didn't say anything, just looked at him, with a long slow smile. 'I understand,' she said, though what she was referring to he didn't know.

Images came clearer now, Ireland, the forty steps at school, remnants of a Georgian past, early mistresses, most of all the poems of Keats and Shelley.

Apart from the priests, there had been things about school he'd enjoyed, the images in poems, the celebration of love and laughter by Keats and Shelley, the excitement at finding a new poem in a book.

She didn't say much to him these days, just looked at him. He was beginning to fall into place, to be whole in this environment of rough and ready young men.

Somehow she had seduced him.

He wore clean, cool, casual white shirts now, looked

faraway at work, hair drifting over his forehead as in adolescence. Someone noticed his clear blue eyes and remarked on them, Irish eyes, and he knew this identification as Irish had not been so absolute for years.

' "They came like swallows and like swallows went," ' Sister Sarah quoted one evening. It was a fragment from a poem by Yeats, referring to Coole Park, a place not far from Liam's home, where the legendary Irish writers convened, Yeats, Synge, Lady Gregory, O'Casey, a host of others, leaving their mark in a place of growth, of bark, of spindly virgin trees. And in a way now Liam associated himself with this horde of shadowy and evasive figures; he was Irish. For that reason alone he had strength now. He came from a country vilified in England but one which, generation after generation, had produced genius, and observation of an extraordinary kind.

Sister Sarah made people do extraordinary things, dance, sing, boys dress as girls, grown men jump over one another like children. She had Liam festoon himself in old clothes, with paper flowers in his hat.

The story of the play ran like this:

Two tinker families are warring. A boy from one falls in love with a girl from the other. They run away and are pursued by Liam who plays King of the Tinkers. He eventually finds them but they kill themselves rather than part and are buried with the King of the Tinkers making a speech about man's greed and folly.

No one questioned that it was too mournful a play for Christmas; there were many funny scenes, wakes, fights, horse-stealing and the final speech, words of which flowed from Liam's mouth, had a beauty, an elegance which made young men from Roscommon who were accustomed to hefty Irish showband singers stop and be amazed at the beauty of language.

Towards the night the play was to run Sister Sarah became a little irritated, a little tired. She'd been working too hard, teaching during the day. She didn't talk to Liam much and he felt hurt and disorganized. He didn't turn up for rehearsal for two nights running. He rang and said he was ill.

He threw a party. All his former friends arrived and Marion's friends. The flat churned with people. Records smashed against the night. People danced. Liam wore an open-neck collarless white shirt. A silver cross was dangling, one picked up from a craft shop in Cornwall.

In the course of the party a girl became very, very drunk and began weeping about an abortion she'd had. She sat in the middle of the floor, crying uproariously, awaiting the arrival of someone.

Eventually, Liam moved towards her, took her in his arms, offered her a cup of tea. She quietened. 'Thank you,' she said simply.

The crowds went home. Bottles were left everywhere. Liam took his coat, walked to an all-night café and, as he didn't have to work, watched the dawn come.

She didn't chastise him. Things went on as normal. He played his part, dressed in ridiculous clothes. Sister Sarah was in a lighter mood. She drank a sherry with Liam one evening, one cold December evening. As it was coming near Christmas she spoke of festivity in Kerry. Cross-road dances in Dún Caoin, the mirth of Kerry which had never died. She told Liam how her father would take her by car to church on Easter Sunday, how they'd watch the waters being blessed and later dance at the cross-roads, melodions playing and the Irish fiddle.

There had been nothing like that in Liam's youth. He'd come from the Midlands, dull green, statues of Mary outside factories. He'd been privileged to know defeat from an early age.

'You should go to Kerry some time,' Sister Sarah said.

'I'd like to,' Liam said, 'I'd like to. But it's too late now.'

Yet when the musicians came to rehearse the music Liam knew it was not too late. He may have missed the west of Ireland in his youth, the simplicity of a Gaelic people but here now in London, melodions exploding, he was in an Ireland he'd never known, the extreme west, gullies, caves, peninsulas, roads winding into desecrated hills and clouds always coming in. 'Imagine,' he thought, 'I've never even seen the sea.'

He told her one night about the fiftieth anniversary of the 1916 revolution which had occurred before he left, old priests at school fumbling with words about dead heroes, bedraggled tricolours flying over the school and young priests, beautiful in the extreme, reciting the poetry of Patrick Pearse.

'When the bombs came in England,' Liam said, 'and we were blamed, the ordinary Irish working people, I knew they were to blame, those priests, the people who lied about glorious deeds. Violence is never, ever glorious.'

He met her in a café for coffee one day and she laughed and said it was almost like having an affair. She said she'd once fancied a boy in Kerry, a boy she was directing in *All My Sons*. He had bushy blond hair, kept Renoir reproductions on his wall, was a bank clerk. 'But he went off with another girl,' she said, 'and broke my heart.'

He met her in Soho Square Gardens one day and they walked together. She spoke of Africa and the States, travelling, the mission of the modern church, the redemption of souls lost in a mire of nonchalance. On Tottenham Court Road she said goodbye to him.

'See you next rehearsal,' she said.

He stood there when she left and wanted to tell her she'd awakened in him a desire for a country long forgotten, an awareness of another side of that country, music, drama, levity but there was no saying these things.

When the night of the play finally arrived he acted his part well. But all the time, all the time he kept an eye out for her.

Afterwards there were celebrations, balloons dancing, Irish bankers getting drunk. He sat and waited for her to come to him and when she didn't rose and looked for her.

She was speaking to an elderly Irish labourer.

He stood there, patiently, for a moment. He wanted her to tell him about Christmas lights in Ireland long ago, about the music of O'Riada and the southern going whales. But she persevered in speaking to this old man about Christmas in Kerry.

Eventually he danced with her. She held his arm softly. He knew now he was in love with her and didn't know how to put it to her. She left him and talked to some other people.

Later she danced again with him. It was as though she saw something in his eyes, something forbidding.

'I have to go now,' she said as the music still played. She touched his arm gently, moved away. His eyes searched for her afterwards but couldn't find her. Young men he'd acted with came up and started clapping him on the back. They joked and they laughed. Suddenly Liam found he was getting sick. He didn't make for the lavatory. He went instead to the street. There he vomited. It was raining. He got very wet going home.

At Christmas he went to midnight mass in Westminster Cathedral, a thing he had never done before. He stood with women in mink coats and Irish charwomen as the choir sang 'Come all ye faithful'. He had Christmas with an old aunt and at midday rang Marion. They didn't say much to one another that day but after Christmas she came to see him.

One evening they slept together. They made love as they had not for years, he entering her deeply, resonantly, thinking of Galway long ago, a river where they swam as children.

She stayed after Christmas. They were more subdued with one another. Marion was pregnant. She worked for a while and when her pregnancy became too obvious she ceased working.

She walked a lot. He wondered at a woman, his wife, how he hadn't noticed before how beautiful she looked. They were passing Camden Town one day when he recalled a nun he'd once known. He told Marion about her, asked her to enter with him, went in a door, asked for Sister Sarah.

Someone he didn't recognize told him she'd gone to Nigeria, that she'd chosen the African sun to boys in black jerseys. He wanted to follow her for one blind moment, to tell her that people like her were too rare to be lost but knew no words of his would convince her. He took his wife's hand and went about his life, quieter than he had been before.

The Sojourner

He lived in a little room in Shepherd's Bush. There was a bed for himself and above a little compartment for visitors. One climbed by ladder to this area. A curtain separated it from the rest of the room. It was this area he'd reserved for Moira.

Around the walls were accumulated Italian masterpieces, pieces of Titian, pieces of Tintoretto, arms by Caravaggio, golden and brusque. Dominating all was a Medici face by Botticelli. Above the fireplace a young man, stern, glassy eyes, his lips satisified, his stare resigned to the darkness of the room, a darkness penetrated by the light of one window.

Jackie worked on a building site. He'd worked on one since he'd come over in February. Previously he'd been a chef in a café in Killarney, riding to and from work on a motorbike. But something made him go, family problems, spring, lust.

The room had been conveniently vacated by two Provisional Sinn Féin members from Kerry. He'd scraped Patrick Pearse from the wall. They were gone to another flat.

He'd risen early on mornings when Shepherd's Bush had been suffocated in cold white fog, a boy from Ireland hugging himself into a donkey jacket. He'd been picked up in a lorry, driven to diverse sites. Now the mornings were warm. Blue crept along the corners of high rise flats, lingering bits of dawn. Jackie was enclosed in a routine, last night's litter outside country and western pubs, Guinness bottles, condoms, the refuse of Ireland in exile. The work was hard but then there was Moira to think of. At odd moments when life was harsh or reality pressing her image veered towards him; as he sat in

the lorry, tightening his fists in the pockets of his donkey
jacket, as he sat over a mug of tea in the site office. Moira
Finnerty was his sister, at present in a mental hospital in
Limerick but shortly to be released. She was coming to
London to stay with him.

Jackie and Moira had grown up on a lowly farm in the
Kerry mountains. Their parents had been quiet, gruff,
physically in love with one another until their sixties. A
grandfather lived with them, always telling indecent stories.
There'd been many geese, cows, a mare always looking in the
direction of the ocean, a blizzard of gulls always blowing over
the fields. Life had been hard. Jackie had gone to school in
Killarney. Moira had attended a convent in Cahirciveen.

Jackie had peddled dope at fifteen in the juke box cafés of
Killarney. His first affair had been at sixteen with the
daughter of a rich American business man, sent to the
convent in Killarney by way of a quirk. After all Killarney was
prettier than Lucerne or Locarno and it was possessed of its
own international community. Sarah was from Michigan,
randy, blonde, fulsome. She'd always had money, a plethora
of nuns chasing her. However she'd avoided the nuns, sat in
jeans, which always looked at though they were about to
explode, in cafés, smoking French cigarettes, smattering the
air with French fumes.

Sex for Jackie until now was associated with the sea;
recalling Sarah he thought more of an intimacy with the sea,
with beaches near Ballinskelligs, inlets with the spire of
Skellig Mhicel in the distance, an odd mound in the sea
where monks once sang Deus Meus, the chants of Gaelic
Ireland before Elizabethan soldiers sailed westwards on
currachs.

Sarah had gone. There'd been many girls, Killarney was
full of girls. He did his Leaving Certificate twice which led to
nights lounging in cafés in Killarney, Valentine cards circulat-
ing from year to year, and one ice-cream parlour in Killarney
where a picture of a Spanish poet stood alongside pictures of
Powerscourt House, County Wicklow, and Ladies' View,

Killarney, one tear dropping out of his eye, rolling up in a little quizzical ball and a bullet wound in his head. It was an odd cartoon to show in a café but then the owners were Portuguese so one accepted the odd divergence more easily.

Jackie had gone to Dublin, worked on building sites, peddled dope; lived like a prince in Rathmines. However, the arm of the law fell upon him. He was imprisoned for six months, returned to Kerry. A good cook, he got a job in a café in a world of provincial Irish cafés, always the juke-box pounding out the bleeding heart of provincial Ireland, songs about long-distance lorry drivers and tragic deaths in Kentucky.

His sister emerged from convent school about this time, got a job in a hospital in Limerick. It was supposed to be temporary but she stayed there. Moira, when she hadn't been at school, had spent her adolescence wandering the hills about their home. There'd been few trees so one could always pick her out. She'd rarely gone to dances and when she had she'd always left early before the other girls, thumbing home.

They rarely spoke, but there was always something there, a mirror-like silence. Jackie saw himself in Moira, saw the inarticulate disparate things, a moment of high on an acid trip in Rathmines, a moment of love in a café in Killarney, a moment of reverie by the sea in Ballinskelligs. The west of Ireland for all its confusion was full of these things and it was these people Jackie veered towards, people who spoke a secret language like the tinkers' Shelta.

You discerned sensitivity in people or you didn't. Jackie was an emotional snob. He was a snob in clothes, in cigarettes, in brands of dope even. But one thing he never minded was working and wending his way among the semi-literate.

Moira had spent two years in Limerick when she had an affair with an older married man. The usual. He made love to her, took every advantage of her shy, chubby body. Then returned to the suburbs. It was more than that which made Moira crack up. Her parents seemed content to leave her, not to expect anything remarkable of her. By solicitude they condemned her to a life of non-achievement.

Jackie had gone by the time Moira was put in the mental hospital in Limerick. Her face pressed on him. At first he thought to go back and rescue her. But he relied on time and patience. Moira was to be let out in June. He wrote and asked her to come and stay with him. For a while.

Early June in Shepherd's Bush, the young of London walked along the street. Bottles flew. Bruce Lee continually played in the cinema. Irish country and western singers roared out with increasing desperation and one sensed behind the songs about Kerry and Cavan, mothers and luxuriant shamrock, the foetus of an unborn child urging its way from the womb of a girl over for a quick abortion.

Sometimes Jackie allowed himself to be picked up. He'd long lost interest sexually in women. The last girl he'd actually wanted to make love to had been in Dublin, a blonde who ran away to a group in California, mystical and foreign to the Irish experience. Walking in Shepherd's Bush was like walking among the refuse of other people's lives, many bins in the vicinity. He read many paperbacks. On colder days he lit fires in his room and sat over them like a tinker. Above the door was a St Brigid's cross which traditionally kept away evil. He'd bought it at the Irish tourist office in Bond Street. There was a desk in his room on which he wrote letters home. He thought of his mother with her giant chamber-pot which had emerald patterns of foliage on it. She'd bought it in an antique shop in Listowel. He thought of his father, a randy look always in his eye. As children they'd hear their parents making love like people in far-off cities in a far-off time were supposed to. He could still distinguish his mother's orgasms, a cry in the air, a siren which was sublimated into the sound of a gull, the sound of a train veering towards Tralee.

They'd only had one another, he and Moira. They'd made the most of it.

Now he wrote to her.

Dear Moira,
Expecting you soon. The weather is changeable here.
The job's hard. I think I may go to Copenhagen in
autumn. See you soon.

> Love,
> Jackie.

She arrived unexpectedly one morning. The doorbell
exploded. He jumped up. Oddly enough he was on the
upper tier. He'd gone up there for a change. He climbed
down the ladder, went to the door. He'd overslept. She was
there, with two cases, scarf on her head, something more
moderate about her face, less of the mysticism.

They kissed. Her breath smelt of Irish mints.

As there was no coffee he made her tea which they had on
the floor. He was late for work but he decided to go anyway
as he was on a nearby site. She'd sleep. He'd be back later.
He bid her goodbye. She lay asleep in the upper bed. Before
closing the door he looked around this den of loneliness.
Moira's slip lay over a chair.

She had the room tidy when he returned and she herself
looked refreshed, having bathed in the grotty bath with its
reverential gas flame bursting into life. Her scent had
changed. There were perfumes of two kinds of soap in it.

This time she made tea and they sat down. He didn't want
to ask her about the mental hospital so instead he queried her
about home. Moira didn't want to talk about home so instead
she imparted gossip about DJs on Irish radio.

Jackie made a meal, one he'd been preparing in his mind
for a long time, lamb curry. Afterwards they had banana
crumble and custard, eating on the floor. Moira said it would
be necessary for her to get a job. Jackie didn't disagree. Moira
read the little pieces of print stuck about. A line from Yeats.
An admonition from Socrates. Soon a point came whereby
there seemed nothing else to talk about so both were silent.

They went for a drink before going to bed. Jackie
apologized for the grottiness of the pub. Moira said she didn't

mind, her eyes drifting about to young Irish men holding their sacred pints of Guinness.

Afterwards they returned through the dustbins and slept in their individual beds.

It being summer Moira got a job in a nearby ice-cream parlour, dressing in white, doling out runny ice-cream to West Indian children. In a generally bad summer the weather suddenly brightened and Jackie was conscious of himself, a young Adonis on a building site. His body had hardened, muscle upon muscle defining themselves. His hair was short. His face more than anything was defined, those bright eyes that shot out, often angry without a reason as though some subconscious hurt was disturbing him.

What he resented was the young Irish students who were arriving on the building site. They brought with them a gossipy closeness to Ireland and a lack of seriousness in their separation from that country. However, he and Moira were getting on exceedingly well. There was less talk of trauma than he'd anticipated. They had drinks, meals, outings together. On Sundays there was Holland Park and Kensington Gardens. They had picnics there. Sometimes they swam in the Serpentine. Moira's head dipped a lot, into magazines, into flowers, into the grass. The vestiges of wardship were leaving. Jackie often felt like knocking back a lock of Moira's hair. Something about her invited these gestures, her total preoccupation with a Sunday newspaper cartoon, her gaze that sometimes went from you and turned inwards, to that area they both held in common.

Moira cooked sometimes. She was a plain cook but a good one. She made brown bread much like his mother's. Jackie's cooking was more prodigious, curries that always scared Moira, lest there be drugs in them, chicken paprika, beef goulash, moussaka, and then the plates of Ireland, Limerick ham glazed in honey, Dublin coddle, Irish stew.

The divisions in the room were neatly made, borders between her area and his. Both were exceptionally neat.

For the first time she mentioned the mental hospital. It

slipped out. There had been a woman there who'd had nine children, whose husband had left her, who scrubbed floors in a café and who'd eventually cracked up. In a final gesture of humiliation she'd wept while mopping the floor one day so that the proprietor reckoned she should see a psychiatrist. 'Jesus, I'm crying. I'm just crying,' she'd shouted. 'I'm just crying because they told me life would be better, men helpful. I'm just crying and I'm not ashamed. I can manage. I can manage myself.' They'd told her she couldn't and quietly stole her children, placing them in homes. It was then she'd cracked up, looking like all the other mad visionary women of Ireland, women who claimed to have seen Maria Goretti in far-flung cottages.

'They force you to crack up,' Moira said, 'so that they can be satisfied with their own lot. After all the idea of pain, real pain, is too big to cope with. Pain can be so beautiful. The pain of recognizing how hopeless things are yet accepting and somehow building from it.'

His sister had grown. More than that she'd become beautiful, her Peruvian eyes calm and often a scarlet ribbon in her hair. Playing a game they'd played as children both of them dressed up at nights and went to showband concerts. Whatever her other sophistications Moira had not relinquished the showband world so they traipsed off to pubs, Moira in a summer dress, Jackie in a suit, a green silk Chinese tie on him, girls from Offaly moaning into microphones. You were scrutinized at the doors lest you were not Irish. Often there was some doubt about Jackie until he opened his mouth. Inside people jostled, a majority of women edged for a man. Lights changed from scarlet to blue and somehow Moira in her dreamy, virginal way, seemed at home here, lost in a reverie of rural Ireland.

Shyness had gone, a kind of frankness prevailed. Often Jackie sat around his room in just trousers. Moira washed in her slip, sometimes it falling over her hips.

'You know we made a pact, didn't we, when we were growing up?' Jackie said one evening. 'Mammy and Daddy never seemed to notice us.'

It was true. Against their parents' carnality they'd chosen a kind of virginal complacency.

Once in Kerry, looking at the moon, Moira had stated that this country had always been a country of nuns. In ancient times nuns had built cottages by nearby beaches.

It was less that they were a nun and a monk, more that they had to resist. Resist their parents' self-absorption, resist the geese, the skies, the dun of the mountains, the purple changing to green of the rocks.

Jackie had had his affairs. In fact Moira had hers. But it was as though they'd made a vow of celibacy when Jackie was thirteen and Moira eleven; they didn't want to fall into the trap of closing themselves off. They wanted to be open, romantic, available. Looking into Moira's eyes before going to bed Jackie saw that in fact they were closing themselves off in a different way.

They were outsiders, resigned to be outsiders and were making a fetish of this role. Moira had picked up a little teddybear in Shepherd's Bush market. In her bed she held it. She was sitting up in her slip. 'Goodnight Jackie,' she said.

The teddybear slept with her.

That night Jackie walked the environs of Shepherd's Bush, sat in a café, spoke to a man from Ghana. He waited some hours. The first light came. He returned home, picked up his things for work, waited for a lorry on Shepherd's Bush Green.

She wanted to dance now so she danced with him. They travelled to Kilburn and Camden. Saturday nights in ballrooms, the London Irish swung to visiting showbands. Despite this venture in a foreign city Moira had a lonesomeness for the decay of rural Ireland, for its fetishes. Jackie dancing with her, cheek to cheek, wondered if he could cure it.

It was a miserable summer weather-wise. Early in August there was a much advertised march against troops in Northern Ireland. Jackie and Moira saw it by accident, young English people shouting about women in Northern Ireland jails.

Later that month the Queen's cousin was blown up in County Sligo. Moira and Jackie didn't listen to the radio much but they heard a jumbled commentary on the events. Jackie wondered about the Provisional Sinn Féin people who'd lived in this room once, that was their domain, instant and shocking deaths in the cause of Ireland. He smiled. No one in the whole of London reprimanded Jackie or Moira but the papers were full of hatred, mistaking the source of the guilt.

The guilt was a shared one Jackie thought, a handed down one. Everyone's hands were dipped in blood; blood of intolerance. He'd thought about it so much, knew the kind of prevalent and often justified anger of Irish republicans. In Kerry they were eccentrics. One IRA man he knew grew the best marijuana in Kerry and decorated it with Christmas decorations come Christmas. Often Northern republicans fled to his house, men with trapped eyes. Reaching to them was like reaching to dynamite. They hit back easily.

So Jackie and Moira assumed responsibility for the deaths of the Earl Mountbatten, the Dowager Lady Brabourne and the two children killed with them. They walked about London with the air of criminals. The newspapers had ordained this guilt. Jackie and Moira accepted it, not as slaves but with a certain grandeur. They were Irish and as such bore a kind of mass guilt, guilt for the republican few, for the order of the gun, the enslaved and frightened eyes, the winsome thoughts of Patrick Pearse. It was all part of their heritage; to deny it would be like denying the wet weather. But in accepting a certain responsibility both knew, Jackie more than Moira, of a more real tradition which never met English eyes, the tradition of the great families of Kerry, the goblets of wine, the harp, the Gregorian chant.

They'd left Kerry with their wolfhounds, going to Europe, but something was always ready to be disturbed of this tradition, a hedge-schoolmaster behind a white hawthorn tree reading Cicero, O'Connell, another Kerryman, in Clontarf telling the Irish proletariat that the freedom of Ireland is not worth the shedding of one drop of blood, Michael Davitt in Clare leading a silent pacifist march against English landlords.

Jackie knew, as all sensitive and knowledgeable Irish people knew, that the prevalent philosophy of Irish history was pacifism and he could therefore accept the rebukes of the English newspapers with glee, with a certain amount of wonder, knowing them to be founded and spread in ignorance.

But Moira wasn't so sure. He'd noticed her fluctuating somewhat. Although outwardly calm there was a new intensity in her dancing. She was going back, quicker than he could cope with, to the ballroom floors in Kerry, the point at which all is surrendered, the days of drudgery, the nights of squalid sex in the backs of cars. She was trying to be peaceful with a violent heritage.

In a dancehall one night there was a fight. Someone hit someone else on the head with a chair. A woman started singing 'God save Ireland said the Heroes' and in moments Jackie's dreams of pacifism were gone. A young man made a speech about H. Blocks on the counter and somewhere an auburn-haired woman described her lust for a Clare farmer.

Jackie took Moira home. She began crying, sitting on a chair.

In moments it was gone, a summer of harmony. The tears came, scarlet, outraged blue. Afterwards it was the silence which was compelling. She was steadily recalling the corners of a mental hospital, the outreaches of pain. Her heart in a moment had turned to stone.

It was a curious stone too which her heart had become, exquisite and frail in its own way. She began going to dances by herself and one night she did not return. Jackie sat up, waiting until the small hours. When there was no sign of her he went out for a while, hugging himself into a donkey jacket. Autumn was coming.

People are like doctors. We live with one another for a while. We cure one another. Jackie saw himself as physician but too late. Moira no longer needed his physician's touch. She was sleeping around, compulsively giving herself, engineering all kinds of romances. And when she stopped talking to him much he too searched the night for strangers. At first unsuccessfully. But then they came, one by one, Argentinians, West Indians.

She perceived the domain of his life, said nothing.

'Pope visits war-torn country,' the papers warned.

It was true, John Paul was coming, giving an ultimate benediction to the dancehalls, the showbands, the neon lights, the juke-boxes that shook jauntily with their burden of song.

He saw the look on Moira's face and knew she was destined to return. Nothing could hold her back. Dancing to an Irish showband singer's version of 'One Day at a Time' he realized her need for the hurt, the intimacy, the pain of ballroom Ireland. She wanted to be immolated by these things.

There was nothing he could say against it. It was his life against hers and she saw his life as a shambles. He couldn't tell her about the boys with diamond eyes, no more than she could tell him about the lads from Cork who jumped on her as though she was an old and unusable mattress. In mid-September she announced her decision.

A bunch of marigolds sat on the mantelpiece, a little throne of tranquillity.

'Will you come too?' she said.

'No,' he said and half-naked he looked at her. He wanted to ask her why it was necessary always to return to the point where you were rejected, but such questions were useless. The Pope was coming, the music of ballroom Ireland was strong in her ears.

He took her to Euston and she asked him if he had any messages for their parents.

'Tell them I won't be home for Christmas,' he said.

She looked at him. Her eyes looked as though they were going to pop out and grapple him and take their mutual pain but they did no such thing.

Later that night Jackie wandered in Shepherd's Bush. He knew he'd deceived himself, going from body to body, holding out hope he'd meet someone who'd fulfil some childhood dream of purity.

All his life he'd been trying to reconstruct her, not so much Moira, as that virgin of Ireland, Our Lady of Knock, Our Lady of the Sorrows, that complacent maiden who edged into juke-box cafés, into small towns where apparitions had taken place in the last century and now neon strove into the rain.

He wouldn't go to Copenhagen. He'd go south. He'd pack up his things and leave, knowing there was a certain compulsion about the sun, the Mediterranean, the shine of the sun on southern beaches.

Before leaving London there was one thing he wanted to do, dress up like any other Irish boy, comb his hair, put on his green Chinese tie and dance until all was forgotten, the lights of Killarney, the whine of the juke-box, the look on Moira's face as she stared over a stone wall in Kerry, into a world which would consume their knowledge of the sea, their knowledge of stone, their reverence of one another.

The Mourning Thief

Coming through the black night he wondered what lay before him, a father lying dying. Christmas, midnight ceremonies in a church which stood up like a gravestone, floods about his home.

With him were his wife and his friend Gerard. They needn't have come by boat but something purgatorial demanded it of Liam, the gulls that shot over like stars, the roxy music in the juke-box, the occasional Irish ballad rising in cherished defiance of the sea.

The night was soft, breezes intruded, plucking hair, thread lying loose in many coloured jerseys. Susan fell asleep once while Liam looked at Gerard. It was Gerard's first time in Ireland. Gerard's eyes were chestnut, his dark hair cropped like a monk on a bottle of English brandy.

With his wife sleeping Liam could acknowledge the physical relationship that lay between them. It wasn't that Susan didn't know, but despite the truism of promiscuity in the school where they worked there still abided laws like the Old Testament God's, reserving carnality for smiles after dark.

A train to Galway, the Midlands frozen in.

Susan looked out like a Botticelli Venus, a little worried, often just vacuous. She was a music teacher, thus her mind was penetrated by the vibrations of Bach even if the place was a public lavatory or a Lyons café.

The red house at the end of the street; it looked cold, pushed away from the other houses. A river in flood lay behind. A woman, his mother, greeted him. He an only child, she soon to be widow. But something disturbed Liam with excitement. Christmas candles still burned in this town.

His father lay in bed, still magically alive, white hair smeared on him like a dummy, that hard face that never forgave an enemy in the police force still on him. He was delighted to see Liam. At eighty-three he was a most ancient father, marrying late, begetting late, his wife fifteen years younger than him.

A train brushed the distance outside. Adolescence return-ed with a sudden start, the cold flurry of snow as the train in which he was travelling sped towards Dublin, the films about Russian winters.

Irish winters became Russian winters in turn and half of Liam's memories of adolescence were of the fantasized presence of Russia. Ikons, candles, streets agleam with snow.

'Still painting?'

'Still painting.' As though he could ever give it up. His father smiled as though he were about to grin. 'Well, we never made a policeman out of you.'

At ten, the day before he would have been inaugurated as a boy scout, Liam handed in his uniform. He always hated the colours of the Irish flag, mixing like the yolk in a bad egg.

It hadn't disappointed his father that he hadn't turned into a military man but his father preferred to hold on to a shred of prejudice against Liam's chosen profession, leaving momentarily aside one of his most cherished memories, visiting the National Gallery in Dublin once with his son, encountering the curator by accident and having the curator show them around, an old man who'd since died, leaving behind a batch of poems and a highly publicized relationship with an international writer.

But the sorest point, the point now neither would mention, was arguments about violence. At seventeen Liam walked the local hurling pitch with petitions against the war in Vietnam.

Liam's father's fame, apart from being a police inspector of note, was fighting in the GPO in 1916 and subsequently being arrested on the Republican side in the civil war. Liam was against violence, pure and simple. Nothing could convince him that 1916 was right. Nothing could convince him it was different from now, old women, young children, being blown to bits in Belfast.

Statues abounded in this house; in every nook and cranny was a statue, a statue of Mary, a statue of Joseph, an emblem perhaps of some saint Mrs Fogarthy had sweetly long forgotten.

This was the first thing Gerard noticed, and Susan who had seen this menagerie before was still surprised. 'It's like a holy statue farm.'

Gerard said it was like a holy statue museum. They were sitting by the fire, two days before Christmas. Mrs Fogarthy had gone to bed.

'It is a museum,' Liam said, 'all kinds of memories, curious sensations here, ghosts. The ghosts of Irish republicans, of policemen, military men, priests, the ghosts of Ireland.'

'Why ghosts?' Gerard asked.

'Because Ireland is dying,' Liam said.

Just then they heard his father cough.

Mr Fogarthy was slowly dying, cancer welling up in him. He was dying painfully and yet peacefully because he had a dedicated wife to look after him and a river in flood around, somehow calling Christ to mind, calling penance to mind, instilling a sense of winter in him that went back a long time, a river in flood around a limestone town.

Liam offered to cook the Christmas dinner but his mother scoffed him. He was a good cook, Susan vouched. Once Liam had cooked and his father had said he wouldn't give it to the dogs.

They walked, Liam, Susan, Gerard, in a town where women were hugged into coats like brown paper accidentally blown about them. They walked in the grounds of Liam's former school, once a Georgian estate, now beautiful, elegant still in the East Galway winter solstice.

There were tinkers to be seen in the town, and English hippies behaving like tinkers. Many turkeys were displayed, fatter than ever, festooned by holly.

Altogether one would notice prosperity everywhere, cars, shining clothes, modern fronts replacing the antique ones Liam recalled and pieced together from childhood.

But he would not forfeit England for his dull patch of Ireland, Southern England where he'd lived since he was twenty-two, Sussex, the trees plump as ripe pears, the rolling verdure, the odd delight of an Elizabethan cottage. He taught with Susan, with Gerard, in a free school. He taught children to paint. Susan taught them to play musical instruments. Gerard looked after younger children though he himself played a musical instrument, a cello.

Once Liam and Susan had journeyed to London to hear him play at St Martin-in-the-Fields, entertaining ladies who wore poppies in their lapels, as his recital coincided with Remembrance Day and paper poppies generated an explosion of remembrance.

Susan went to bed early now, complaining of fatigue, and Gerard and Liam were left with one another.

Though both were obviously male they were lovers, lovers in a tentative kind of way, occasionally sleeping with one another. It was still an experiment but for Liam held a matrix of adolescent fantasy. Though he married at twenty-two, his sexual fantasy from adolescence was always homosexual.

Susan could not complain. In fact it rather charmed her. She'd had more lovers since they'd married than fingers could count; Liam would always accost her with questions about their physicality; were they more satisfying than him?

But he knew he could count on her; tenderness between them had lasted six years now.

She was English, very much English. Gerard was English. Liam was left with this odd quarrel of Irishness. Memories of adolescence at boarding school, waking from horrific dreams nightly when he went to the window to throw himself out but couldn't because window sills were jammed.

His father had placed him at boarding school, to toughen him like meat.

Liam had not been toughened, chastened, ran away twice. At eighteen he left altogether, went to England, worked on a building site, put himself through college. He ended up in Sussex, losing a major part of his Irishness but retaining this, a knowledge when the weather was going to change, a premonition of all kinds of disasters and ironically an acceptance of the worst disasters of all, death, estrangement.

Now that his father was near death, old teachers, soldiers, policemen called, downing sherries, laughing rhetorically, sitting beside the bed covered by a quilt that looked like twenty inflated balloons.

Sometimes Liam, Susan, Gerard sat with these people, exchanging remarks about the weather, the fringe of politics or the world economic state generally.

Mrs Fogarthy swept up a lot. She dusted and danced around with a cloth as though she'd been doing this all her life, fretting and fiddling with the house.

Cars went by. Geese went by, clanking terribly. Rain came and church bells sounded from a desperate steeple.

Liam's father reminisced about 1916, recalling little incidents, fights with British soldiers, comrades dying in his arms, ladies fainting from hunger, escape to Mayo, later imprisonment in the Curragh during the civil war. Liam said: 'Do you ever connect it with now, men, women, children being blown up, the La Mon Hotel bombing, Bessbrook killings, Birmingham, Bloody Friday? Do you ever think that the legends and the brilliance built from your revolution created this, death justified for death's sake, the stories in the classroom, the priests' stories, this language, this celebration of blood?'

Although Liam's father fought himself once, he belonged to those who deplored the present violence, seeing no connection. Liam saw the connection but disavowed both.

'Hooligans! Murderers!' Liam's father said.

Liam said, 'You were once a hooligan then.'

'We fought to set a majority free.'

'And created the spirit of violence in the new state. We were weaned on violence, me and others of my age. Not actual violence but always with a reference to violence. Violence was right, we were told in class. How can one blame those now who go out and plant bombs to kill old women when they were once told this was right?'

The dying man became angry. He didn't look at Liam, looked beyond him to the street.

'The men who fought in 1916 were heroes. Those who lay bombs in cafés are scum.'

Betrayed he was silent then, silent because his son accused him on his death-bed of unjustifiably resorting to bloodshed once. Now guns went off daily, in the far-off North. Where was the line between right and wrong? Who could say? An old man on his death-bed prayed that the guns he'd fired in 1916 had been for a right cause and in the words of his leader Patrick Pearse had not caused undue bloodshed.

On Christmas Eve the three young people and Mrs Fogarthy went to midnight mass in the local church. In fact it wasn't to the main church but a smaller one, situated on the outskirts of the town, protruding like a headstone.

A bald middle-aged priest greeted a packed congregation. The cemetery lay nearby, but one was unaware of it. Christmas candles and Christmas trees glowed in bungalows.

'Come all ye Faithful,' a choir of matchstick boys sang. Their dress was scarlet, scarlet of joy.

Afterwards Mrs Fogarthy penetrated the crib with a whisper of prayer.

Christmas morning, clean, spare, Liam was aware of estrangement from his father, that his father was ruminating on his words about violence, wondering were he and his ilk, the teachers, police, clergy of Ireland responsible for what was happening now, in the first place by nurturing the cult of violence, contributing to the actuality of it as expressed by young men in Belfast and London.

Sitting up on Christmas morning Mr Fogarthy stared

ahead. There was a curiosity about his forehead. Was he guilty? Were those in high places guilty like his son said?

Christmas dinner; Gerard joked, Susan smiled, Mrs Fogarthy had a sheaf of joy. Liam tidied and somehow sherry elicited a chuckle and a song from Mrs Fogarthy. 'I have seen the lark soar high at morn.' The song rose to the bedroom where her husband who'd had dinner in bed heard it.

The street outside was bare.

Gerard fetched a guitar and brought all to completion, Christmas, birth, festive eating, by a rendition of Bach's 'Jesu, Joy of Man's Desiring.'

Liam brought tea to his father. His father looked at him. ''Twas lovely music,' his father said with a sudden brogue, 'there was a Miss Hanratty who lived here before you were born who studied music at Heidelberg and could play Schumann in such a way as to bring tears to the cat's eyes. Poor soul, she died young, a member of the ladies' confraternity. Schumann was her favourite and Mendelssohn came after that. She played at our wedding, your mother's and mine. She played Mozart and afterwards in the hotel sang a song, what was it, oh yes, ''The Star of the County Down.''

'Such a sweetness she had in her voice too.

'But she was a bit of a loner and a bit lost here. Never too well really. She died maybe when you were a young lad.'

Reminiscences, names from the past, Catholic names, Protestant names, the names of boys in the rugby club, in the golf club. Protestant girls he'd danced with, nights at the October fair.

They came easily now, a simple jargon. Sometimes though the old man visibly stopped to consider his child's rebuke.

Liam gauged the sadness, wished he hadn't said anything, wanted to simplify it but knew it possessed all the simplicity it could have, a man on his death bed in dreadful doubt.

Christmas night they visited the convent crib, Liam, Susan, Gerard, Mrs Fogarthy, a place glowing with a red lamp.

Outside trees stood in silence, a mist thinking of envelop-

ing them. The town lay in silence. At odd intervals one heard
the gurgle of television but otherwise it could have been
childhood, the fair green, space, emptiness, the rhythm, the
dance of one's childhood dreams.

Liam spoke to his father that evening.

'Where I work we try to educate children differently from
other places, teach them to develop and grow from within,
try to direct them from the most natural point within them.
There are many such schools now but ours, ours I think is
special, run as a co-operative; we try to take children from all
class backgrounds and begin at the beginning to redefine
education.'

'And do you honestly think they'll be better educated
children than you were, that the way we educated you was
wrong?'

Liam paused.

'Well, it's an alternative.'

His father didn't respond, thinking of nationalistic, com-
radely Irish school-teachers long ago. Nothing could convince him that the discipline of the old style of education
wasn't better, grounding children in basic skills.

Silence somehow interrupted a conversation, darkness
deep around them, the water of the floods shining, reflecting
stars.

Liam said goodnight. Liam's father grunted. Susan already
lay in bed. Liam got in beside her. They heard a bird let out a
scream in the sky like a baby and they went asleep.

Gerard woke them in the morning, strumming a guitar.

St Stephen's Day, mummers stalked the street, children
with blackened faces and a regalia of rags collecting for the
wren. Music of a tin whistle came from a pub, the town
coming to life. The river shone with sun.

Susan divined a child dressed like old King Cole, a crown
on her head and her face blackened. Gerard was intrigued.
They walked the town. Mrs Fogarthy had lunch ready. But
Liam was worried, deeply worried. His father lay above,
immersed in the past.

Liam had his past, too, always anxious in adolescence, running away to Dublin, eventually running away to England. The first times home had been odd; he noticed the solitariness of his parents. They'd needed him like they needed an ill-tended dog.

Susan and he had married in the local church. There'd been a contagion of aunts and uncles at the wedding. Mrs Fogarthy had prepared a meal. Salad and cake. The river had not been in flood then.

In England he worked hard. Ireland could so easily be forgotten with the imprint of things creative, children's drawing, oak trees in blossom. Tudor cottages where young women in pinafores served tea and cakes home made and juiced with icing.

He'd had no children. But Gerard now was both a twin, a child, a lover to him. There were all kinds of possibility. Experiment was only beginning. Yet Ireland, Christmas, returned him to something, least of all the presence of death, more a proximity to the prom, empty laburnum pods and hawthorn trees naked and crouched with winter. Here he was at home with thoughts, thoughts of himself, of adolescence.

Here he made his own being like a doll on a miniature globe. He knew whence he came and if he wasn't sure where he was going, at least he wasn't distraught about it.

They walked with his mother that afternoon. Later an aunt came, preened for Christmas and the imminence of death. She enjoyed the tea, the knowledgeable silences, looked at Susan as though she was not from England but a far-off country, an eastern country hidden in the mountains. Liam's father spoke to her not of 1916 but of policemen they'd known, irascible characters, forgetting that he had been the most irascible of all, a domineering man with a wizened face ordering his inferiors around.

He'd brought law. He'd brought order to the town. But he'd failed to bring trust. Maybe that's why his son had left. Maybe that's why he was pondering the fate of the Irish revolution now, men with high foreheads who'd shaped the fate of the Irish republic.

His thoughts brought him to killings now being done in the name of Ireland. There his thoughts floundered. From where arose this language of violence for the sake and convenience of violence?

Liam strode by the prom alone that evening, locked in a donkey jacket.

There were rings of light around distant electric poles.

He knew his father to be sitting up in bed; the policeman he'd been talking about earlier gone from his mind and his thoughts on 1916, on guns, and blazes, and rumination in prison cells long ago.

And long after that thoughts on the glorification of acts of violence, the minds of children caressed with the deeds of violence.

He'd be thinking of his son who fled and left the country.

His son now was thinking of the times he'd run away to Dublin, to the neon lights slitting the night, of the time he went to the river to throw himself in and didn't, of his final flight from Ireland.

He wanted to say something, urge a statement to birth that would unite father and son but couldn't think of anything to say. He stopped by a tree and looked to the river. An odd car went by towards Dublin.

Why this need to run? Even as he was thinking that, a saying of his father returned: 'Idleness is the thief of time.' That statement had been flayed upon him as a child but with time as he lived in England among fields of oak trees that statement had changed; time itself had become the culprit, the thief.

And the image of time as a thief was forever embroiled in a particular ikon of his father's, that of a pacifist who ran through Dublin helping the wounded in 1916, was arrested, was shot dead with a deaf and dumb youth. And that man, more than anybody, was Liam's hero, an Irish pacifist, a pacifist born of his father's revolution, a pacifist born of his father's state.

He returned home quickly, drew the door on his father. He sat down.

'Remember, Daddy, the story you told me about the pacifist shot dead in 1916 with a deaf and dumb youth, the man whose wife was a feminist?'

'Yes.'

'Well, I was just thinking that he's the sort of man we need now, one who comes from a revolution but understands it in a different way, a creative way, who understands that change isn't born from violence but intense and self-sacrificing acts.'

His father understood what he was saying, that there was a remnant of 1916 that was relevant and urgent now, that there had been at least one man among the men of 1916 who could speak to the present generation and show them that guns were not diamonds, that blood was precious, that birth most poignantly issues from restraint.

Liam went to bed. In the middle of the night he woke muttering to himself, 'May God have mercy on your soul', although his father was not yet dead but he wasn't asking God to have mercy on his father's soul but on the soul of Ireland, the many souls born out of his father's statelet, the women never pregnant, the cruel and violent priests, the young exiles, the old exiles, those who would never come back.

He got up, walked down the stairs, opened the door of his father's room. Inside his father lay. He wanted to see this with his own eyes, hope even in the persuasion of death.

He returned to bed.

His wife turned away from him but curiously that did not hurt him because he was thinking of the water rising, the moon on the water and as he thought of these things geese clanked over, throwing their reflections into the water grazed with moon which rimmed this town, the church towers, the slate roofs, those that slept now, those who didn't remember.